THE TWILIGHT ZONE

• A Novel •

Nona Fernández

Translated from the Spanish by Natasha Wimmer

Graywolf Press

Originally published in 2016 as *La dimensión desconocida* by Penguin Random House Grupo Editorial, Santiago

Dialogue and title from *The Twilight Zone* courtesy of CBS Broadcasting, Inc.

"The Dark Room" by Enrique Lihn, translated by David Unger, from *The Dark Room and Other Poems*, copyright © 1963, 1972 by Enrique Lihn, © 1978 by Enrique Lihn and David Unger. Reprinted by permission of New Directions Publishing Corp.

"We Didn't Start the Fire." Words and Music by Billy Joel. Copyright © 1989 JOELSONGS. All Rights Administered by ALMO MUSIC CORP. All Rights Reserved Used by Permission. Reprinted by Permission of Hal Leonard LLC.

This publication is made possible, in part, by the voters of Minnesota through a Minnesota State Arts Board Operating Support grant, thanks to a legislative appropriation from the arts and cultural heritage fund. Significant support has also been provided by Target Foundation, the McKnight Foundation, the Lannan Foundation, the Amazon Literary Partnership, and other generous contributions from foundations, corporations, and individuals. To these organizations and individuals we offer our heartfelt thanks.

MINNESOTA
STATE ARTS BOARD

CLEAN
WATER
LAND &
LEGACY
AMENDMENT

Published by Graywolf Press
250 Third Avenue North, Suite 600
Minneapolis, Minnesota 55401

All rights reserved.

www.graywolfpress.org

Published in the United States of America

ISBN 978-1-64445-047-5

2 4 6 8 9 7 5 3 1
First Graywolf Printing, 2021

Library of Congress Control Number: 2020937613

Cover design: Walter Green

THE TWILIGHT ZONE

Also by Nona Fernández in English

Space Invaders

For M, D, and P
my most important letters

Contents

Beyond the known world there is another dimension.

You've just crossed over.

THE TWILIGHT ZONE

I imagine and give voice to old trees,
the cement under my feet,
the stale air circling this place.

I imagine and complete unfinished stories,
reconstruct half-told tales.

I imagine and bring to life the traces of gunfire.

ENTRY ZONE

I imagine him walking down a city street. A tall man, thin, black hair, bushy mustache. In his left hand is a folded magazine. He grips it tightly, seeming to draw strength from it as he walks. I imagine him in a hurry, smoking a cigarette, glancing nervously from side to side, making sure no one is following him. It's the month of August. Specifically, the morning of August 27, 1984. I imagine him going into a building at Calle Húerfanos and Bandera. The editorial offices of *Cauce* magazine. I'm not imagining that part; I read it. The receptionist recognizes him. He's come before with the same request: he needs to talk to the reporter who wrote the article in the magazine he's carrying. I have a hard time imagining the woman at the reception desk. I can't form a clear picture of her, not even her expression as she eyes the nervous man before her, but I'm sure she's wary of him and his urgency. I imagine she tries to put him off, tells him the person he wants isn't here and won't be in all day, there's no point waiting, he should leave and not come back, and I also imagine—because that's my role in this story—a female voice interrupting the scene. A voice I can imagine as I write, if I close my eyes.

It's me you want, the voice says. How can I help you?

The man studies the woman speaking to him. Probably he knows all about her. He must have seen a picture of her at some point. Maybe he tailed her once or read her file. She's

7

the person he wants. The one who wrote the article he read and brought with him. He's sure of it. Which is why he approaches her and extends his right hand, offering her his armed forces ID card.

I imagine the reporter wasn't expecting anything like this. She looks at the card in bewilderment—and fear, I might add. Andrés Antonio Valenzuela Morales, Soldier First Class, ID #39432, district of La Ligua. Accompanying this information is a photograph stamped with the registration number 66650. I'm not imagining that part either, I'm reading it right here, in a statement later written by the same reporter.

I want to tell you about some things I've done, says the man, looking her in the eye, and I imagine his voice shaking slightly as he speaks these words, which aren't imagined. I want to tell you about making people disappear.

The first time I saw him was on the cover of a magazine. It was a copy of *Cauce*, the kind of thing I read back then with no knowledge of the people featured in all those headlines reporting attacks, kidnappings, strikes, crimes, scams, lawsuits, indictments, and other scandalous occurrences of the day. "Accused Bomber Was Local CNI Boss," "*Degollados* Killers Still Doing Time in La Moneda," "The Plot to Assassinate Tucapel Jiménez," "Did DINA Order Calama Executions?" My reading of the world at thirteen was shaped by stories in magazines I didn't own, that belonged to everybody, passed from hand to hand among my classmates. The pictures in each issue gradually arranged themselves into a confusing landscape that I never managed to map in its entirety, though each dark detail lingered in my dreams.

I remember a scene I came up with in my head after reading some article. On the cover of the magazine was a drawing of a blindfolded man in a chair. An agent was interrogating him in the glare of a lamp. Inside the magazine was a catalog of torture methods. I read the testimonies of victims and saw diagrams and drawings that looked like something out of a book from the Middle Ages. I can't remember every detail, but clear in my mind is the story of a sixteen-year-old girl who said that in the detention center where she was kept they had stripped her, smeared her body with excrement, and put her in a dark room full of rats.

I didn't want to, but inevitably I imagined that dark room full of rats.

I often dreamed of that place and woke up from the dream over and over.

Even now I can't shake it and maybe that's why I'm recording it here, as a way to let it go.

In that same dream, or maybe another like it, I inherited the man I'm imagining. An ordinary man, no different from anyone else, nothing special about him. Except for a bushy mustache, which I, at least, couldn't stop thinking about. His face was on the cover of one of those magazines, and over the picture was a headline in white letters: I TORTURED PEOPLE. Under that, another line: SHOCKING EYEWITNESS ACCOUNT BY SECURITY SERVICES AGENT. In a pull-out section inside there was a long exclusive interview. The man gave a full account of his time as an intelligence agent, from his service as a young conscript in the air force to the moment he went to the magazine to tell his story. There were pages and pages of details about what he had done: the names of agents, prisoners, informers; detention center addresses, burial sites, descriptions of torture methods; accounts of many missions. Powder blue pages—I remember them well—transporting me for a moment into some parallel reality, infinite and dark as the room I dreamed of. A disturbing universe that we sensed lay hidden somewhere out there, beyond the bounds of school and home, where everything obeyed a logic governed by captivity and rats. A horror story told by the ordinary person at its center, who looked like our science teacher, or so it seemed to us, with the same bushy mustache. The man who tortured people didn't mention any rats in the interview, but he could have been the tamer of them all. I guess that's what I imagined. A pied piper playing a tune that made it impossible not to follow him, not to march one by one into the disturbing place he inhabited. He didn't seem like a monster or an evil giant, or some psychopath you had to run away from. He didn't even look like the national police in boots, helmet, and shield who charged at us with batons during street protests. The man who tortured people could have been anybody. Even our teacher.

The second time I saw him was twenty-five years later. I was working as a writer for a television series, and one of the main characters was based on him. It was a fictional series with lots of romance, of course, which is a requirement on TV, plus plenty of persecution and death, in keeping with the subject matter and the period.

The character we constructed was an intelligence agent who took part in detention and torture operations and then went home and listened to a mix tape of love songs and read Spiderman comics with his son at bedtime. For twelve episodes we followed his double life up close, the absolute divide between the personal and the professional that was secretly crushing him. He wasn't comfortable in his job anymore, he was starting to lose his nerve, the tranquilizers had stopped working, he couldn't eat or sleep, he had stopped talking to his wife, stopped being affectionate with his son, stopped spending time with his friends. He felt sick, despairing, feared his superiors, was trapped in a reality he didn't know how to escape. At the climax of the series he put himself in front of his own enemies, presenting them with the brutal testimony of what he'd done as an intelligence agent in a desperate gesture of catharsis and unburdening.

To write the series I had to confront the interview I'd last read as an adolescent.

There he was again, on the cover.

His bushy mustache, his dark eyes staring at me from the page, and that line printed over his photograph: I TORTURED PEOPLE.

The spell remained intact. His face loomed again, and like a rat I was ready to follow wherever his testimony led. I pored over every word. Twenty-five years later my hazy map was gradually coming into focus. Now I had a clear sense of the identity and roles of the people whose names and nicknames he mentioned. Air Force Colonel Edgar Ceballos Jones; Air Force Intelligence Director General Enrique Ruiz Bunger; Communist Party leader José Weibel Navarrete; Communist Party member Quila Rodríguez Gallardo, known for his bravery; El Wally, civilian officer of the Joint Command; El Fanta, ex–Communist Party member turned informer and persecutor; El Fifo Palma, Carlos Contreras Maluje, Yuri Gahona, Carol Flores, Guillermo Bratti, René Basoa, El Coño Molina, Mr. Velasco, El Patán, El Yerko, El Lutti, La Firma, Peldehue, Remo Cero, Nido 18, Nido 20, Nido 22, the Juan Antonio Ríos Intelligence Center. The list is endless. I reentered that dark zone, but this time with a lamp that I had been fueling for years, which made it easier for me to find my way once I was inside. The lamp lit my path, and I became convinced that every bit of information delivered by the man who tortured people had been put out there not just to shock readers and open their eyes to the nightmare, but also to halt the machinery of evil. It was clear and concrete proof, a message from the other side of the looking glass, genuine and incontrovertible, demonstrating that the whole of that parallel and invisible universe was real, not some fantastic invention, as was often said.

I last saw him a few weeks ago. I'd been working on the script for a documentary by some friends. It was about the Vicariate of Solidarity, an agency of the Catholic Church created in the midst of the dictatorship to assist victims. The film was a record of counterintelligence work, carried out mostly by the agency's lawyers and social workers. From testimonies and material collected for each case of forcible disappearance, detention, abduction, torture, and any other abuses they handled, they were able to put together a kind of panorama of repression. By obsessively studying this landscape, the Vicariate team tried to expose the sinister logic at work in the hope of getting a step ahead of the agents and saving lives.

We'd been working on the film for years and the material was so intense it made us a little queasy. My friends, the creators of the documentary, recorded hours and hours of interviews. Each person described on camera how they joined the Vicariate, their work, and the strange way they gradually became detectives, spies, secret investigators. They all ended up analyzing information, asking questions, planning operations, building a mirror image of the enemy's security services, but to nobler ends. The interviews were utterly engrossing and thorough, making the editing process very difficult. Which is why I had to make sure to prepare for our meetings first thing in the morning, with a strong cup of coffee so that I was as sharp as possible.

I want to describe one such morning. Shower, coffee, notebook, pencil, and then pushing the Play button to queue up new material to review. As I watched I took notes, paused images, tested cuts in my head, listened over and over to clips in order to decide whether they were necessary or not. That's where I was, in the middle of testimonies, interviews, and stock images viewed millions of times, when he appeared: the man who tortured people.

There he was in front of me, no longer just a still image printed in a magazine.

His face came to life onscreen, the old spell was revived, and for the first time he was in motion. His eyes blinked on camera, his eyebrows shifted a little. I could even see the slight rise and fall of his chest as he breathed.

My friends explained to me that while he was briefly back in Chile they had managed to secure an interview. He hadn't been back since he snuck out of the country after giving his testimony in the eighties. Thirty years later he had returned to appear in court and present further evidence, this time to a judge or multiple judges. It was his idea; he hadn't been summoned. Even the French interior ministry and the agents charged with his safety all these years had tried to dissuade him. What I saw on my screen that morning was the image of a man who had come home after a long time, hoping to bring a chapter to a close. In fact, he said as much in the only interview he gave to the press at the time.

As I write now, I pull up the image on my screen again.

It's him. There he is, on the other side of the glass.

The man who tortured people looks me in the face as if it's really me he's talking to. He has the same bushy mustache, but it's no longer black; it's closer to gray, like his hair. Thirty years have gone by since that photograph on the cover of *Cauce* magazine. Thirty years, betrayed by the wrinkles furrowing his brow, his tinted glasses, the now-gray hair. He's speaking in a voice I've not heard before. It's a calm voice, very different from what it must have been when he turned up to give testimony in eighty-four. Soft and timid, even; nothing like what I had imagined. It's as if he's answering my friends' questions despite himself, reluctantly, but with the conviction that it's his duty, as though he's following orders.

I look at him and consider that: the secret compulsion to be constantly obeying some superior.

Now it's all just part of an old story, and he keeps repeating the phrase "I remember" as his eyes reveal the workings of memory. Only a few moments from the interview capture my attention. Things I haven't read elsewhere, spoken calmly, released into the air for me to gather and write down.

I remember the first marches.

People came out with posters of disappeared family members. Sometimes I walked past them.

I saw those women, those men.

I looked at the photographs they were carrying and I said to myself: they don't realize that I know where that person is, I know what happened to him.

My face is reflected in the television screen and my face merges with his. I see myself behind him, or maybe in front of him. I look like a ghost in the picture, a shadow lurking, a spy watching him though he doesn't know it. Which is partly what I am now, as I sit here observing him, I think: a spy watching him though he doesn't know it. He's so close I could whisper in his ear. Pass on some message he would mistake for a thought of his own, because he doesn't see me, doesn't know I'm here, intent on speaking to him. Or writing to him, actually, which is the only thing I know how to do. It could be a couple of sentences on the screen that he'll read like a ghostly apparition before his eyes. A sign from beyond the grave, which is something he must be used to. A message in a glass bottle tossed into the black sea where all those who ever lived in that dark parallel zone are shipwrecked. It won't be easy, but I'll get his address and write him a letter, in an attempt to make contact. The letter will be perfectly formal, using phrases like *dear sir, I am writing to you, sincerely yours,* because that's the only way I imagine he'd ever read it. In it I'll tell him I want to write about him and I think it's only right to let him know, and maybe, if he's interested, make him part of a project I have in mind.

Dear Andrés,

We don't know each other, and I hope my boldness in tracking down your address and taking the liberty to write won't stop you from reading this letter. The reason I want to be in touch is that I have dreamed of writing a book about you. Why? Good question, and indeed I've wondered as much myself without finding a satisfactory answer. I can't explain it exactly, because the source of my obsessions is never clear, and, over time, that's what you've become for me: an obsession. Without realizing it, I've been following you since I was thirteen years old, when I saw you on that *Cauce* magazine cover. I didn't understand everything that was happening around me when I was a girl—I still don't—and I suppose that, in my attempt to understand back then, I was captivated by your words, by the possibility of using them to decipher the enigma. Later, for work, and because I was interested, I came to know your story in greater detail and I read everything about it that I could get my hands on, which still seems paltry and insufficient given the value of the information you provided. Now, writing to you, I'm trying again to clarify my motives so that I sound less vague, but the honest truth is that all I can come up with are more questions.

Why should I write about you? Why should I resurrect a story that began more than forty years ago? Why bring up curved knives, electric shock torture, and the rats again? Why bring up the disappearances? Why should I talk about a man who was part of it all and at some point decided he couldn't be anymore? How do you decide when you've had enough? What kind of line do you cross? Is there such a line? Is the line the same for all of us? What would I have done if, like you, I had reported for military service at eighteen, and my superior had sent me to guard a group of political prisoners? Would I have done my job? Would I have run away? Would I have understood that this was the beginning of the end? What would my partner have done? What would my father have done? What would my son do in the same place? Does someone have to take that place? Whose images are these in my head? Whose screams? Did I read about them in the testimony you gave the reporter or did I hear them myself somewhere? Are they part of a scene from your life or mine? Is there some fine line that separates collective dreams? Is there a place where you and I both dream of a dark room full of rats? Do these images creep into your mind, too, and keep you awake? Will we ever escape this dream? Will we ever emerge and give the world the bad news about what we were capable of doing?

When I was a girl, I was told that if I misbehaved the man with the sack would come for me. All disobedient children disappeared into that wicked old man's bottomless dark sack. But rather than frighten me, the story piqued my curiosity. I secretly wanted to meet the man, open his sack, climb into it, see the disappeared children, and get to the heart of the terrible mystery. I imagined it many times. I gave him a face, a suit, a pair of shoes. When I did, he became more disturbing, because normally the face I gave him belonged to someone I knew: my father, my uncle, the corner grocer, the mechanic next door, my science teacher. Any of them could be the old man with the sack. Even I could probably play the part, if I looked in the mirror and drew on a mustache.

Dear Andrés, I'm the woman who wants to look into the sack.

Dear Andrés, I'm the woman who's ready to draw on a mustache to play you.

If you've read this far and my request doesn't seem absurd or inappropriate, I'd be grateful if you'd write to me at this address. I eagerly await your response.

The alarm goes off at 6:30 every morning. What follows is a long chain of hurried, awkward acts, an attempt to start the day by shooing away sleep, to forge ahead while yawning and wanting to go back to bed. Drawers opening, cups filling with coffee and milk, taps turning. Showers, toothbrushes, deodorant, combs, toast, butter, the morning news, the announcer reporting the latest carjacking or the day's gridlock. Heating lunch for my son, putting it in a thermos, making a snack for recess. And between each rushed activity, calls of hurry up, it's late, let's go. The cat meows, it wants food and water. The garbage truck goes by, taking away the trash we put out last night. The school bus stops in front and honks for my neighbors. The children come out yelling, their mother sees them off. The man with the dog goes by with his dog and waves as I'm opening the gate and my son's father is starting the car, getting ready to leave. The young man who jogs is jogging. The woman with the cell phone is talking on her cell phone. Everything is just like yesterday or the day before yesterday or tomorrow, and in the spatiotemporal cycle that we move in daily, my son gives me a kiss to complete the ritual, gets in the car with his father, and the two leave at exactly 7:30 so as not to break the protective spell.

It's been like this for years.

We began the routine when my son was little. In those

days we didn't have a car, and each morning I said goodbye to him as he walked out the door to nursery school, holding his father's hand. I kissed him and hugged him tight because secretly I was panicked that I might never see him again. Terrifying thoughts assailed me each time we parted. I imagined a bus barreling into him, a live wire dropping from electric poles onto his head, a mad dog coming out of a house and lunging for his neck, some pervert picking him up from nursery school, the man with the sack kidnapping him and never bringing him back. The possibilities were dramatic and infinite. My fearful new-mother's brain fabricated horrors, and in that unhinged exercise, each time he came home was a gift.

With time, the madness came to an end. I no longer dream up calamities, but during that morning departure ritual I always focus on the image of my son and his father as they're leaving. It's a snapshot suspended in my mind until I see them again. An uncontrollable impulse that I inherited from those days as a frightened new mother, the distillation of an archaic fear that I suppose we all have and try to keep under control, the fear of unexpectedly losing the people we love.

I don't know what the morning routine must have been like at the Weibel Barahona household in 1976. I was just four years old and I can't even remember what my own mornings were like back then, but with a little imagination I can see that house in La Florida and the family beginning their day. I doubt their routine was much different from the one I follow daily with my family, or the one that all families with children in this country have been following daily for years. I imagine the Weibels' clock marking the launch time, maybe 6:30, the same as ours here. I imagine José and María Teresa, the parents, jumping out of bed and delegating the morning tasks. One makes breakfast, the other gets the children out of bed; one helps them get dressed, the other ushers them into the bathroom; one heats up the lunches, the other prepares the snacks; one is in charge of calling hurry up, it's late, let's go. A perfect, well-oiled machine, probably better oiled than ours, because there were two children in the Weibel Barahona household in 1976, not one, like in ours, so their morning maneuvers must sometimes have acquired heroic proportions.

On March 29, 1976, at 7:30 a.m., the same time my son and his father leave the house each day, José and María Teresa left to take their children to school. They waited at the bus stop nearby with one of their neighbors, who in my mind's eye has the face of the man who walks his dog each morning in my neighborhood. In all likelihood they greeted each other, as they probably did each morning, just as the man with the dog and I nod at each other when he passes by each day, the two of us planting the flag of everyday normality, tracing the fine line of our protective routine. At 7:40, as part of their own daily ritual, the Weibel Barahonas got on a bus on the Circunvalación Américo Vespucio line, which would take them to their destination. The bus was probably full. I can't know that with certainty, but I assume it was, because at that time of day buses all across the country are full, no matter the decade. María Teresa sat in the front seat with one of her children on her lap. Maybe José sat next to her holding their other child. Or maybe he didn't. Maybe he remained standing, moving as close to his family as possible so as not to be separated from them, not to break the threads that keep them safe within rescue distance.

José and María Teresa don't talk about it in front of the children, but this apparently normal morning isn't exactly that. José's brother disappeared a few months ago and he himself, a high-ranking member of the Communist Party, knows he is being watched. Yesterday a young man they didn't recognize rang the doorbell to ask about a washing machine that was supposedly for sale. José and María Teresa know the significance of this strange and disturbing visit, so they've decided to leave their beloved house on Calle Teniente Merino in La Florida this very day. The children don't know it, but they're about to be dropped off at school and at the end of the day home may be somewhere else.

I imagine José and María Teresa ride in silence. They are both tense, and probably don't feel like talking. I imagine they answer their children's questions, stay engaged in the conversation, but inside they're wondering what the future holds for them. They're probably watching the faces of the people around them. Surreptitiously they look out for suspicious glances, threatening gestures. They're on the alert, but it's hard to keep track of everything going on. There are lots of people on the bus at this hour, lots of people getting on and paying the fare. Lots of people walking past and sitting down and falling asleep. Lots of people standing. Lots of people looking out the window. So even though they do their best, they don't spot him in the crowd. Even when their gazes meet, they don't see him.

It's him, the man who tortured people.

Armed forces intelligence agent Andrés Antonio Valenzuela Morales, registration number 66650, Soldier First Class, ID

#39432 of the district of La Ligua. Tall, thin, black-haired, with a dark, bushy mustache.

He sits at the back of the bus. He wears a hidden radio transmitter to communicate with the vehicles following them unseen. Nearby is El Huaso, with El Álex a few seats away, then El Rodrigo. Each agent has gotten on separately, mingling with the passengers, and now they're watching the Weibel Barahonas unnoticed.

But maybe they are noticed. Maybe José lets his gaze linger for a moment on the dark eyes of the man who tortured people. Maybe he sees something troubling in those eyes, something he doesn't have time to process, because just then a woman screams, startling everyone. Somebody stole my purse, she says, and as she speaks, three cars cut off the bus.

Then things happen very quickly. Six men get on through the back and front doors. El Álex and El Huaso shout that it's José who snatched the purse. That's the bastard, they say, and they point at José, who barely understands what's happening, though he's beginning to have an idea. The Weibel Barahona children look at their father in bewilderment. He's been with them all this time, near, very near, never breaking the threads that keep the family within rescue distance, so he can't have taken anyone's purse. And anyway, he's their father, the man who gets them out of bed every morning, who takes care of them, who brings them to school. He's no thief. But it doesn't matter what the children think, because the man who tortured people and his companions approach José, point a gun at him, and say they're police and he's under arrest for robbery. It doesn't matter that José has no allegedly stolen purse, or that María Teresa is crying and pleading for help because she knows exactly what's happening. It doesn't matter that the children are scared, that the bus driver doesn't understand what's going on, that the passengers are watching in fear. The man who tortured people and his companions shove José out the door and in less than a minute they've put him in one of their cars and he's gone forever.

I wonder whether José took a mental snapshot of his family in that instant. I wonder whether he managed to catch a last glimpse of his wife and children from the car, freezing the protective image. My runaway sentimental imagination wants to believe that he did, and that the image helped him keep terror at bay in the gray realm where he was condemned to spend the last days of his life.

In the privacy of the *Cauce* magazine offices, the reporter listened to that story. It was one of the first related to her by the man who tortured people. I can imagine the moment perfectly. He: sitting in an office chair, still nervous, ill at ease. She: listening from behind the desk with a tape recorder running. The words of the man who tortured people are being recorded on tape that is turning and turning in the machine, as the reporter's imagination begins to run away with her, as mine does, staging the scenes that emerge from his testimony. José riding in the car with a group of unidentified agents. The bus with his family in it fading into the distance behind them, getting smaller and smaller until it disappears, severing the threads that keep the family within rescue distance . . . The reporter can finish the rest of the story herself, because she knew José, they were close friends, and she's heard María Teresa describe the same scene on the bus from her own perspective. Now, in 1984, eight years later, neither María Teresa nor the children nor the reporter know what's happened to José.

Envoy from the dark side, guide to that secret dimension, the man who tortured people said José was taken to a command center on Calle Dieciocho called La Firma. The man who tortured people said José was taken straight to an interrogation cell. The man who tortured people said José's interrogation was one of the harshest of the era. The man who tortured people said that even so they failed to discover that José was the Communist Party's second in command. The man who tortured people said that later José was taken to the house where he himself and all the unmarried agents slept. José was there for nearly a week, along with other detainees. The man who tortured people said that one night when he was on leave they took José away and disappeared him. The man who tortured people wasn't there, but being familiar with such procedures, he guessed that José was taken to the Cajón del Maipo in the foothills of the Cordillera Central, handcuffed, blindfolded, and then shot and killed. The man who tortured people guesses that they then cut off his fingers at the first joint to make identification more difficult, and they tied stones to his feet with wire and threw him into the river.

The reporter cried when she heard this story.

Her weeping was captured on the tape turning and turning in the cassette recorder.

Like the man who tortured people, I wasn't there when José was killed. But unlike him, it's hard for me to imagine the details of executions at which I wasn't present. I don't know how many people took part, or what they said to each other. I don't know the details of what unfolded. Nor do I want to. I lack the words and images to write the rest of this story. Any attempt I might make to account for the private last moments of someone about to disappear will fall short.

What did José do? What did he hear? What did he think? What was done to him?

Expelled from the realm of that imaginary unknown, powerless to express myself in a language beyond my command, all I know is that there are other easier things for me to imagine. Things outside that dark zone, things I can cradle like a light to better follow this map. Things like that snapshot I want to believe José kept in his memory. In it, María Teresa and his two children are sitting on the bus carrying them to school. The children are in their uniforms with their book bags and their lunch boxes holding the snacks recently prepared. In the photograph they're all smiling. Nothing bad has happened yet, the rescue distance threads are intact, and they're all safe, talking about some random thing, enjoying their last moment together without knowing that's what it was.

I imagine José sees this snapshot in his mind's eye and focuses on it that night at the Cajón del Maipo. As the man who tortured people imagined, José must be blindfolded, his hands bound, and he must be lying on the ground or perhaps standing, facing his executioners. In this last scene in the dark of the mountain night, I imagine the snapshot of the Weibel Barahonas and the sound of machine gun fire aimed at José's back or chest.

The protective spell is broken, his body is tossed into the river, and he disappears forever.

No rescue from any distance is possible in this exercise.

Not even my runaway imagination can do a thing about that.

The opening ceremony for the Museum of Memory and Human Rights was held in January 2010. Attending were the four presidents of the Concertación, the coalition of political parties leading what analysts call the Transition, the period in which reconciliation and justice within the realm of the possible was the official stance. In those years, the decibel level of memories of violence was lowered so that a politics of consensus could be forged to keep the peace. Democracy was still in the custody of the military, with General Pinochet himself as commander in chief of the army and then a senator in Congress, so it was unwise to use the immediate past as a weapon of debate.

When I had to explain the Transition process to my son—on our first visit to the Museum of Memory, as it happens—this was how I explained it, concisely, simply, so that his young mind could understand. When I told him that the person responsible for everything he had just seen in the museum was one of the men who made the laws that governed the country, he looked at me in puzzlement and started to laugh, assuming I was kidding. At ten, my son was already wise to the bad jokes of Chilean history.

Many people were there, twenty years after democracy had been restored. Government officials, the museum's board of directors, family members of victims, journalists, international guests, the general public, and, as I said, those four presidents of the Concertación: Patricio Aylwin (1990–1994), Eduardo Frei (1994–2000), Ricardo Lagos (2000–2006), and the sitting president, Michelle Bachelet (2006–2010). Bachelet stepped forward and took the microphone to give a heartfelt inaugural speech, opening the doors of this legitimized version of our recent memory to the audience and all of Chile. She spoke of a united country, of the hate that had once divided us, and of the need to live together in peace. And there she was, delivering an emotional speech to an equally emotional audience, when two women unexpectedly scaled one of the light towers in the courtyard where the ceremony was being held and shouted that the Concertación administrations, including all of the public figures present, had systematically violated human rights.

How is a museum of memory curated?

Who chooses what to show? Who chooses what to leave out?

The two women shouting at the opening ceremony are Ana Vergara Toledo, sister of Rafael and Eduardo Vergara Toledo, young men killed during the dictatorship, and Catalina Catrileo, sister of deceased Mapuche activist Matías Catrileo. Before the startled members of the audience, Ana pleads for justice for her dead brothers and for political prisoners, and Catalina addresses the president, saying that her brother had been killed a few years before by a national police agent during Bachelet's own administration.

An uncomfortable moment follows. The guests watch uneasily as the president tries to address the women, who continue to challenge her from the light towers, rejecting the proto-col of ceremonies, agreements, consensus, the whole no-tion of polite discourse that has prevailed for so many years. Ana and Catalina's shouting begins to rouse the attendees. Memories of past and current abuses mesh, defying for a brief moment the passivity of museum displays. The women's cries awaken memory, set it in conversation with the pres-ent, raise it from the crypt, and breathe life into it, resusci-tating a creature fashioned from scraps, from bits of different people, from fragments of yesterday and today. The monster wakes and announces itself with an uncontainable howl, tak-ing everyone by surprise, shaking those who thought they were comfortable, problematizing, conflictualizing, provok-ing. And this is the dangerous primal state in which it should remain. That's what I thought when I watched a clip of what happened online, and that's what I'm thinking today as I visit the museum yet again.

I've been here many times. The first time was with my son and mother right after it opened. My son ran around the wide expanse of the central courtyard while my mother looked at everything, surprised by the brightness of the place, the big windows, its resemblance to a contemporary art museum rather than a cemetery or something lugubrious and terrible, as we had imagined. Once inside, we went through the exhib-its painstakingly, reading all the texts, putting on the head-phones to listen to the recorded testimonies, pushing the buttons on the consoles, playing the videos, watching each screen that appeared before us.

We visited all the floors. We went into the September

Eleven Zone, the Fight for Freedom Zone, the Absence and Memory Zone, the Demand for Truth and Justice Zone, the Return of Hope Zone, the Never Again Zone, the Children's Suffering Zone. We saw the *parrilla*, a metal bed frame where electric current was used to shock detainees, and the door of the former public prison. We saw the watchtower of the Calle República detention and torture center, and the cross from Patio 29, a mass grave at the cemetery where many unidentified bodies ended up, and also photographs of various crimes. All of this in no particular order, with little regard for firsts or nexts, because when the subject is horror, the logic of the machinery doesn't much matter. Dates and time lines and causes and effects and explanations are subtleties you might as well skip. The crimes all merge together. A couple of lines for bombings, a few each for throat slashings, death by burning, shootings, firing squads. And causes and effects, as I said, don't appear in any account. It's all one big massacre, a fight between good guys and bad guys who are easy to tell apart because the bad guys are in uniform and the good guys are civilians. There is no in between. There are no accomplices, nobody else is implicated. The citizenry is free of responsibility, innocent, blind, all of them victims. And at each station we cried, of course we did. And then at the next one we were angry, of course we were. And then at the next one we cried again, only to move on and make room for those behind us who were enacting the same ritual of tears and anger, tears and anger, on a kind of emotional roller coaster ride terminating in the End of Dictatorship Zone, where a big blowup of ex-president Patricio Aylwin giving his inaugural address makes visitors' spirits soar, leaving them exultant with joy and hope, more at ease, more at peace, because from now on we're safe, the good guys won, history is forgiving, we'll forget that it was Aylwin himself who went to the military to request a coup in 1973, a fact that isn't part of this chain of memories, and moving on, listening to the happy slogans of democracy's return which inform us that this is the end, everyone's free to go now, and enjoy a refreshing Coca-Cola in the café, or stop by the little souvenir shop—as we do, why not?—to buy a couple of Allende buttons and a postcard of La Moneda in flames.

The second and third time I visited, it was to find material for a couple of projects. I went to the research department, a sort of library of videos, recordings, books, articles, magazines, and other sources, where kind people kindly assist you and point you in the direction of what you're looking for.

Now, on my fourth trip to the museum, I've come to find out something about the man I'm trying to imagine. I know I won't encounter him in the halls of this little outpost of the past. He's not easily labeled good or evil, black or white. The man I'm imagining inhabits a more mixed-up place, awkward and hard to classify, and maybe that's why there's no room for him within these walls. Still, I fantasize that the testimony he gave will turn up here as valuable material for the good guys, in one of the good guy display cases. That photograph on the cover of *Cauce* magazine and the terrible declaration nobody had made before: I TORTURED PEOPLE.

I wander through the museum's various zones on freedom, hope, struggle, justice, truth, reconciliation, solidarity, and other nice words until I come upon a collection of magazines under glass, accompanied by a large display label that reads "Government Suppresses Opposition Magazines. Photographs Banned." This is from a newspaper article that appeared twelve days after the man who tortured people gave his testimony to the *Cauce* magazine reporter. The article describes a court order that forbade certain magazines from publishing anything but text. Accordingly, the magazines on display in the museum feature white boxes on their covers, ghost images that serve only to draw one's attention and rouse suspicion.

What the display fails to explain is that just a few days before this ludicrous measure was adopted, publication of five issues of *Cauce* magazine had been suspended. Objections were raised and a grievance filed, and after some back and forth, the courts ruled in the magazine's favor. Then the government made another bumbling attempt at censorship, and that's what I'm seeing now exhibited on the museum's walls. A new plea was made for legal protection. Since *Cauce* magazine had been victorious in court before, it seemed likely that the ruling would be favorable, but in November 1984, nearly two months after the man who tortured people gave his testimony, a state of siege was reported in the *Diario Oficial*, under which the publication of *Cauce* magazine was banned completely. The government was resorting to the only unbeatable weapon it had left: the suspension of civil rights.

This long, tortuous road of harassment, bans, censorship, and so forth is obviously directly related to the testimony that the man who tortured people gave to the reporter. And yet that isn't recorded here in the museum; it's like one of those blank magazine covers, an invisible, off-script story, something that perhaps exists only inside my head as I seek a central role for the man I'm trying to imagine.

I imagine the reporter listening to the man as he gives a detailed account of the kidnapping, torture, and death of many of her dear friends. I imagine the contradictory feelings that must have rocked her as she listened to his long testimony. Urges to strangle him, scratch him, hit him, yell at him, but with the simultaneous conviction that she could do none of those things. I know—I'm not imagining—that he was prepared to confess everything and then go back to headquarters to let his superiors do whatever they wanted to him. I know—I'm not imagining—that *whatever* meant death. I know—I'm not imagining—that he didn't care. Anything would be better than the anguish he felt. Better than getting up and going to bed with the smell of death, as he put it. The reporter convinced him that his suicidal plan made no sense. She told him to think of his children, to give himself a chance. She offered him protection. She would get in touch with people who could help him. I know—I'm not imagining—that he mulled it over, that he smoked many cigarettes, probably thinking about his children, as the reporter had suggested, or his wife, or some possible future. I know—I'm not imagining—that he accepted the offer of protection and from that moment he put himself in the hands of people who could help him. I know—I'm not imagining—that he didn't go back to headquarters, that his absence was noticed, and with the passage of time his superiors realized what had happened.

Beyond that, I know nothing. All the rest is the work of the imagination.

Police and military agents scour the country for the disappeared Andrés Valenzuela Morales. Frantic, desperate, frustrated, enraged. Fucking deserter, motherfucking squealer, they must have shouted, waiting to find him and eliminate him, take him to the Cajón del Maipo, cut his fingers off at the first joint, throw him into the river. And as they were hunting for him, they tried to block the publication of his testimony, full of too many secrets. Magazines were banned, photographs censored, and a state of siege declared in order to prevent the circulation of the opposition press, out of fear that the story would open the door to the dark zone, that ultimate portal of evil and stupidity.

There is a section of the museum that I like the best. Well, everybody likes it best because it was designed to seduce visitors, even spoilsports like me. Guides describe it as the heart of the museum. From an observation platform surrounded by candles, which aren't actually candles but little bulbs, more than a thousand photographs of many of the regime's victims are visible, hung high up on one wall. The photographs were donated by the victims' families, so we see them at home, at celebrations, at the beach, smiling at the camera the way we all do when we want to leave a record of ourselves at our best. There are beautiful women who look like movie stars, who must have fixed themselves up flirtatiously, thinking they'd give the photo to a boyfriend, a lover. There's a young man dressed in a tuxedo and bow tie, ready for some big event or likely in the middle of one. He looks happy, elated. There's a man on the beach, holding his son's hand. There's another man with his arms around people who aren't fully visible, as if on some outing or picnic in the country. There's a woman with her mouth open, captured midlaugh. There's another serious-looking woman, shy in front of the camera. They're all snapshots, like the pictures I keep of my son, my father, my mother, my friends, the people I love. Protective, luminous images that foster connection despite death and the passage of time. Seen together, they look like a big family. In a way, they are. Uncles and aunts, brothers and sisters, nephews and nieces, cousins, grandparents, people related by extreme circumstances. There is a touch screen in the middle of the observation platform that you can click on to search for people and learn how they were arrested and killed.

I click and search for José Weibel.

His photograph appears onscreen. He wears glasses and has a gentle smile. He's looking off to one side, probably at someone talking to him, in the middle of a calm, trusting conversation. I try to imagine the scene, but then I stop myself. I've gone too far already, I think. There's no need to imagine more. The text that appears on the screen about his detention and assassination comes mostly from the account of the man who tortured people. The information reproduced here is not attributed to him.

I click and search for Carlos Contreras Maluje.

Carlos stares out at me from the screen. He is also wearing thick glasses. It's a small picture and all you can see is his face, like in an ID photo. But it's still possible to extrapolate the big, broad-shouldered frame described in the testimony of the man who tortured people. I read in Carlos's profile that he was a pharmacist and that he had been city councilman for Concepción. I read in his profile that he was arrested twice. The second time was on Calle Nataniel, just a few blocks from the house where I lived as a girl. Again, the text that appears on the screen about his detention and death comes mostly from the confession of the man who tortured people. Again, it's unattributed.

I click and search for Quila Leo, known for his bravery.
    I click and search for Don Alonso Gahona.
    I click and search for René Basoa.
    I click and search for Carol Flores.

Many of the names I've read in the testimony of the man who tortured people come into focus on this screen, acquire a face, an expression, the spark of life. Even if it's a virtual life, an extension of the photographs hanging on this transparent, celestial wall like a piece of the sky. Or better yet, a piece of outer space where all the faces swallowed up by some twilight zone swim, lost, like untethered astronauts.

This door we unlock with the key of the imagination. Behind it we find another dimension. Ladies and gentlemen, you're about to enter a secret world of dreams and ideas. You're about to enter the twilight zone.

In the seventies, sitting in front of a black and white television set in the kitchen of my old house, I watched episode after episode of *The Twilight Zone*. I'd be lying if I said that I remember the series in detail, but I'm forever marked by that seductive feeling of disquiet and the narrator's voice inviting viewers into a secret world, a universe unfolding outside the ordinary, beyond the bounds of what we were used to seeing. The short episodes told fantastical, bizarre stories. A man with a stopwatch that can stop time. A man who sees gremlins that hound him and try to bring down the plane he's in. A man who is reunited with his ten-year-old son, while in a parallel world that is considerably more real, the boy is a soldier who dies in battle. A man who talks to his stepdaughter's killer doll. A man who crosses over to the other side of the mirror. In every episode a door or a tiny crack opened, offering a glimpse through the TV screen of an alternate reality that I was eager to visit.

At night my mother got home from work and we ate together. According to her, often I would tell her the story of some episode that had made an impression on me. Apparently she was rarely sure which stories were part of the series and which I had made up. After dinner we went straight to bed, only to leave for school first thing the next day. I can't remember much of our morning routine, or those early years of school, but I know that at noon my mother would come for me once class was finished and bring me home for lunch. We talked during the meal, and after dessert and hot tea with lemon verbena from the patio, she returned to work while I was left in the middle of those long seventies afternoons, *The Twilight Zone* marking the moment when the sun began to set.

A space traveler has to make an emergency landing on an unknown planet a million miles from home. His spaceship is out of commission. His right arm is broken, his forehead cut and bleeding. Colonel Cook, voyager across the ocean of space, will never fly the smoldering wreck of his ship again. He survived the crash, but his lonely journey has just begun. Hurting and afraid, he sends messages home pleading for someone to rescue him, though that appears to be impossible. His people can't come for him and he'll be left all alone, on a small planet in space, his very own twilight zone.

And so a new episode brings the day to a close.

Once, while we were eating lunch, my mother told my grandmother and me about something very strange she had just seen. At noon, right there on Calle Nataniel, a few blocks from our house, a man had thrown himself under the wheels of a bus. It hadn't been an accident. The man was walking along the sidewalk when suddenly he flung himself on purpose, fully aware of what he was doing. The bus screeched to a halt. The passersby who witnessed it froze in confusion, silent and still, as if the stopwatch man on *The Twilight Zone* had scheduled a few minutes of paralysis. A national police jeep pulled up. My mother described how an officer got out and tried to take charge of the situation. She and a group of people had gathered to see what condition the injured man was in. He was big, maybe thirty years old, bleeding heavily from a head wound. He was half-conscious, his eyes barely open, looking around in confusion, as the bus driver tried to explain to the national police officer what had happened.

I can't remember my mother's story very well. She herself sees a blur of images when she tries to reconstruct the scene. She says that as the passersby and the driver and the national police officer were shouting, a group of people moved decisively toward the injured man, who was still on the ground. As soon as he saw them, he yelled as if he'd seen the devil or a pack of gremlins hounding him. He said they were intelligence agents, and they were going to take him away to torture him again, and could he please be left to die in peace, and could a message please be taken to the Maluje pharmacy in Concepción. My mother says that then everyone froze again. The magic stopwatch did its work, and the fear that someone else would land in the hands of the gremlins halted all possibility of reacting. A car drove up, and amid shouts and pleas and kicks and shoves they maneuvered the man into it, who then vanished forever outside the bounds of reality.

My mother doesn't know it, but that morning she was very close to the man who tortured people.

Part of the garbled story that she told and keeps telling at my request is a part of what he relayed to the reporter in his testimony.

The man who tortured people said that Carlos Contreras Maluje had been caught the day before, betrayed by one of his comrades. The man who tortured people said that Maluje was being held at the command center on Calle Dieciocho known as La Firma, and that he was interrogated and tortured late into the night. The man who tortured people said that Carlos Contreras Maluje had declared that the next day he had a point of contact on Calle Nataniel. That if they let him go and he kept the appointment they could arrest one more Communist. The man who tortured people said that they did exactly that. The next day they dropped him off on Calle Nataniel, and Carlos Contreras Maluje walked toward Avenida Matta, shadowed by agents deployed through the neighborhood. The man who tortured people said that he himself was seven blocks away when suddenly, over the radio, he heard another agent say: The subject threw himself under a bus.

The passersby, the people on the street, my mother, the bus driver, everyone inhabiting the surface world of everyday life, were brief witnesses to the crack through which the twilight zone appeared. The man who tortured people said that when he got to the location in question, a crowd had already gathered and it wasn't easy to remove Contreras Maluje, who was shouting, and who, despite being seriously injured, was big and fought hard. Contreras Maluje was then taken back to headquarters on Calle Dieciocho where he was locked up, accused of being a liar, and beaten all day. The man who tortured people said that Contreras Maluje was taken that night to Melipilla, where he was shot and buried in a ditch.

My mother knew none of this when she told us what she'd seen that morning, a few hours before. It took me years to connect her story to the one I read in the testimony of the man who tortured people. While we were having lunch that day, eating the casserole or stew my grandmother had made, Carlos Contreras Maluje was probably getting beaten in a cell on Calle Dieciocho, a few blocks from my old house. While we were helping ourselves to gelatin and drowning it in condensed milk, a dessert we loved, Carlos Contreras Maluje was probably sending telepathic messages to his family and friends, asking someone to come and rescue him from the small, lonely planet where he had landed. That place where he was stranded, afraid and in pain, with no ship to take him back to his home above the Maluje Pharmacy in Concepción.

Hello? Ground Control? Is anybody out there? Can anybody hear me?

Desperate cries, calls for help that no one could answer. While my mother was drinking lemon verbena tea and while I listened to the end of the story of her disturbing experience, Carlos Contreras Maluje was probably bleeding on the floor of his cell, besieged by gremlins, in a time frozen by the deadly stopwatch marking the bounds of the twilight zone. A reality so different, according to the old voice-over, you can only unlock it with the key of the imagination.

I click and search for Andrés Valenzuela Morales's name.

I know I won't find it. This is the Absence and Memory Zone, not the Torturers Who Turn Over a New Leaf Zone, not the Deserters Zone, not the Feelings of Remorse Zone, not the Motherfucking Traitors Zone. The man I'm imagining hasn't died, and he isn't catalogued as a victim. A black hole swallowed him up just like everybody else, and if I want to find him, it can only be here, in front of this screen like something in a control tower, a radio whose signal reaches that eerie planet. The only zone that has no place in this museum.

Dear Andrés, Control Tower here. Are you there? Can you hear me?

Dear Andrés Antonio Valenzuela Morales, Soldier First Class, ID #39432 of La Ligua, Control Tower speaking. Are you there? Can you hear me?

I want to believe it's possible, that my voice can reach that place. That from some still-functioning speaker in your wrecked and broken spaceship you can hear me and maybe even be cheered by my words. I want to believe that your microphone short-circuited and that's why I can't hear what you have to say to me. I want to believe that each time I ask whether you can hear me, you answer yes, that although history and memory have abandoned you in that nebulous place, you're still alive, still standing, still waiting for someone to come and rescue you.

I believe that evil is directly proportional to idiocy. I believe that the territory you roamed in anguish before you disappeared is ruled by idiots. It isn't true that criminals are masterminds. It takes a vast amount of stupidity to assemble the parts of such grotesque, absurd, and cruel machinery. Pure brutality disguised as a master plan. Small people, with small minds, who don't understand the abyss of the other. They lack the language or tools for it. Empathy and compassion require a clear mind. Putting yourself in someone else's shoes, changing your skin, adopting a new face: these are all acts of genuine intelligence.

Dear Andrés, I think you were ultimately an intelligent man.

Each time you vomited after watching an execution. Each time you shut yourself in the bathroom after a torture session. Each time you snuck someone a cigarette or saved an apple from your lunch for a prisoner. Each time you passed on a message to someone's family. Each time you cried. Each time you wanted to speak up but couldn't. Each time you spoke up. Each time you repeated your testimony to reporters, lawyers, judges. Each time you hid. Each time you fled out of fear of being found. Each and every time, each and every day, you used and use your lucid intelligence against the stupidity of where you landed.

You imagined being someone else. You chose to be someone else. You chose.

Being stupid is a personal choice and you don't have to wear a uniform to employ that evil talent. If only you knew, dear Andrés, the number of good guys these days who aren't good and never were, though they have yet to be memorialized in a museum; the number of heroes who aren't heroes and never were. I wonder how we'll tell ourselves the story of our times. Who we'll leave out of the Nice Zones in the story. Who we'll entrust with control and curatorship.

Colonel Cook, space traveler, shipwrecked on that mysterious planet, receives a final radio message from home. In it, his superiors inform him that they can't come to rescue him because a great war has broken out. Good guys and bad guys blowing each other to bits. Everything he knew as his world is beginning to disappear. Any real memory of the past will be preserved solely in Colonel Cook's mind. From now on it will be his mission to record and bear witness to a past that no longer exists. Stranded in captivity on a small planet in outer space—or the twilight zone, as it seems to Colonel Cook—he sends messages into the void about a world that has disappeared.

El Negro was there, El Yoyopulos, El Pelao Lito, El Chirola.
I was the only one from Papudo, which is how I got my name.
And it stuck. Papudo.
I don't know whether I liked being called that or not.
It wasn't the kind of thing I asked myself back then.
I was a kid, I had just enlisted, I never complained.
Nobody calls me that anymore.

Chile isn't so clear in my mind now, I'm forgetting it. But not
Papudo.
Sometimes it all comes back to me. Not the person I was, but
the place.
The sea. The smell of the beach and the black sand sticking
to my toes.
And the taste of clams.

CONTACT ZONE

Once again I imagine him walking down a city street. He's a tall man, thin, black hair, that bushy mustache. He's wearing the same clothes he had on in the photograph in *Cauce* magazine, I think: a checkered shirt and a denim jacket. This time I don't imagine him smoking. He has his hands in his pockets, maybe because of the cold this August afternoon in 1984. He's already seen the reporter. He's just left her office and now he has a new objective. With him is another man who seems to be leading the way. They're heading toward a plaza. Specifically, the Plaza Santa Ana, between Calle Catedral and Calle San Martín. People are everywhere. Passersby on their way from one place to another, like them. I imagine him scanning each face, staring anxiously and trying to guess which among them is his next contact. That man who seems to be waiting for a bus, or that man reading the newspaper on a bench, that man talking on the phone in a booth, that man eating *sopaipillas* with hot sauce at the stand in the middle of the plaza. Or someone else, could be anyone.

His companion stops at the corner. In a low voice, he tells the man who tortured people to keep walking, that in a few feet, at a certain spot in the plaza, someone will be waiting for him. I imagine the man follows instructions. I imagine from the distance he spies a discreet signal from his new contact. A dark man with short hair and a mustache, watching him from behind a pair of sunglasses. He looks like a detective, though he isn't. I imagine the man who tortured people walks casually toward him, rousing no suspicions. Once they meet, the contact turns and gestures for the man to follow him to a car, with no word of greeting or any exchange at all. It's a Renault van, parked with a driver inside. I imagine they walk toward it calmly and get in as anyone might, as if they've known each other forever, as if they're trained in the act of simulation. I imagine once they're inside their eyes meet for the first time, in recognition.

I'm a lawyer at the Vicariate. I know who you are and I know what you told them at the magazine, says the new contact. Or that's what I imagine he says, as the man who tortured people listens, surrendering himself to the situation. And I know our time is short, so let's head straight to the places you mentioned in your testimony.

I imagine the man doesn't question this. I imagine he nods. Because this is precisely what he's chosen to do: talk, show, testify. To the reporter. To this lawyer; to whoever wants to listen while there's still time. And yet the question comes out of his mouth, a tiny act of rebellion. Or maybe exhaustion. Sheer exhaustion.

Now?

Now, says the lawyer as the driver starts the van.

A little while ago, the documentary I worked on about the Vicariate of Solidarity was released. I was traveling abroad, so I wasn't there for the premiere. I was sorry not to get to meet the characters who had for some time occupied my computer screen and taken over my very life. By the end, their faces and voices had become more than familiar to me. I'd spent hours listening to them and trying to find the key to their stories. I would have recognized them on the street if I saw them, whereas they had no idea who I was or how many hours I'd spent spying on them.

Now that I'm back I'll see the film in the theater. I've watched the final cut, but I want the experience of seeing it on the big screen, in Dolby Surround Sound, sitting in a comfortable seat and maybe eating a bag of popcorn—why not? I invite my mother to join me for a noon screening. It's the only showing she can make, so I pick her up and we walk into the Hoyts La Reina Cinema like any other pair of moviegoers, hiding our secret connection to the film we'll be seeing.

A motley lineup is playing. *Avengers 2: Age of Ultron* fills almost all the theaters in assorted versions and at assorted times: 2-D dubbed versions, 2-D subtitled versions, 3-D dubbed versions, 3-D original-language versions, 4-DX dubbed and subtitled versions, and so on, to satisfy each and every special desire to see this band of superheroes. In the movie, supervillain Ultron, assisted by an army of ultrabad guys, tries to destroy humanity. He's challenged by the Avengers, who do their best to save the world. Iron Man, Hulk, Captain America, Black Widow, Thor, Hawkeye, Scarlet Witch, and other Marvel notables I can't recall are the heroes. One character's super speed is complemented by another's super vision, or super strength, or super intelligence, or super humor, or super sex appeal. They work together, they're good-looking, they're fun, they're smart, and though it isn't easy, they do save the planet. I saw the movie with my son a few weeks ago at a screening jam-packed with shrieking kids and teenagers accompanied by adults like me happy to tag along and watch Robert Downey Jr. or Mark Ruffalo fighting for justice. It's always exciting to see attractive people fighting for justice.

Other titles on the marquee are *The Seventh Dwarf, Fast and Furious, Mall Cop, Cinderella, The Second Best Exotic Marigold Hotel, The Cobbler.* Nearly squeezed off the edge of the electronic display of current attractions, we manage to find the documentary's paltry three daily showings. We pay for our tickets, buy a couple of cortados, and go into the theater to see the 1:00 p.m. show, while the rest of the world is eating or making lunch.

An army of red seats constitutes the lonely, unsettling landscape inside the theater. A distinct smell suffuses the space, of Forest Pine or some other air freshener. Left behind are the bright lobby posters, ads for ice cream, deals on drinks and popcorn, video games, pizza menus, ATMs, sound tracks of trailers for coming attractions. As if we were crossing over to the dark side of the moon, the smallest theater in the multiplex awaits us, completely empty and utterly silent. Our steps slow to the pace of a different time inside. It's a dense, plodding time, far from the rain of stimuli that we've just weathered on the other side of the door. We advance through the gloom, looking for seats. The screen is still dark, so all we hear are our voices trying not to disturb the hush. We settle down in the middle of the theater and wait for the show to start with the strange feeling that we're being watched. Probably by the operator in the projection room. Or maybe by someone on the other side of that enormous blank screen.

I remember a certain episode of *The Twilight Zone.* In it an older actress retreats alone to the living room of her mansion to watch, over and over, the movies she acted in when she was younger. She is trying desperately to stop time, and nothing and no one can pry her from her seclusion as she drinks whiskey and watches her own past projected on the screen in the darkness. Outside is the effervescent city of Los Angeles, her old friends, her assistant, her loyal agent trying to find her new job prospects. Scene of a woman watching a screen. Leading lady from long ago, bright star of a vanished constellation, left behind as the earth turns and time passes, intones the announcer as the episode begins. Barbara Jean Trenton, her world a room where dreams are spun of celluloid, struck down by the years and left lying on the sad street, grasping for the license number of fugitive fame.

More than the announcer's intense introduction to the story, it's the memory of Barbara drinking whiskey as she sits before the continuous projection of her past that creeps into my mind in the middle of this empty place. Except for my mother next to me in this theater that is at once tiny and vast, I'm as alone as Barbara. And like her I'm here to watch yet again the same old images that have hounded me for years.

After a few previews the documentary begins. The clatter of a typewriter comes over the theater's speakers. A giant blank sheet of paper appears onscreen and keys type the title of the movie across it. Next comes the bombing of La Moneda yet again, the military proclamations yet again, the National Stadium and the detainees yet again.

Unlike Barbara Jean Trenton, I'm not the protagonist of what I see. I wasn't there, I have no dialogue or part in the plot. The scenes projected in this theater aren't mine, but they've always been close, at my heels. Maybe that's why I think of them as part of my story. I was born with them planted inside me, images in a family album that I didn't choose or arrange. What little I remember from that time are these scenes. In the rapid succession of events that I inhabit, in the whirlwind of images that I consume and discard daily, they stand untouched by time and forgetting. As if governed by a different gravitational force, they neither float away nor spin off into space at random. They're always there, unshakeable. They come back to me or I come back to them, in a dense, circular time, the kind I'm breathing in this empty theater.

I've spent much of my life scrutinizing these images. I've followed their scent, tracked them, collected them. I've inquired about them, requested explanations. I've peered into their corners, their darkest crannies. I've blown them up and sorted them, trying to find a place and a meaning for them.

I've turned them into quotes, proverbs, maxims, jokes. I've written books about them, articles, plays, TV scripts, documentaries, and even soap operas. I've seen them projected on countless screens, printed in books, newspapers, magazines. I've researched them to the point of boredom, imagining or even inventing what I can't understand. I've photocopied them, stolen them, consumed them, displayed and overdisplayed them, exploiting them in every possible way. I've ransacked every page of the album they inhabit, searching for clues that might help me decipher their message. Because I'm sure they, like a black box, hold a message.

In the documentary, one of the subjects talks about the discovery of a mass grave in 1978. A peasant came to the offices of the Vicariate to deliver a valuable piece of information. In an abandoned limestone mine near Santiago, in the district of Isla de Maipo, he said that he had seen a group of hidden bodies. Immediately a commission of lawyers, priests, and reporters set out discreetly to verify the man's claims. When they arrived they made their way into the dark vault of the mine, lighting their way with a torch. As they were combing through the rubble, a human rib cage fell on one of them, confirming the information they had been given. Then they looked up and discovered that the chimneys of the kilns were sealed with bars and wire mesh, concealing a jumble of bones, clothing, lime, and cement. There were fifteen bodies hidden in the mine.

It wasn't easy to find out whose bodies they were. After a long investigation, with the help of expert reports and information accumulated in the Vicariate's archives, it was possible to determine that the exhumed bodies matched a group of people who had been arrested in October 1973. After years spent looking for living loved ones, horrified family members identified the unearthed bodies, putting an end to any hopes of reunion. All the stories they had made up in the face of absence and emptiness began to fall apart, fantasies in which the disappeared parents, siblings, or children were on a desert island, safe, hidden somewhere in the world waiting for the right moment to send word or return. This discovery was the first evidence that prisoners who had yet to appear had likely been killed. From that point on, families and professionals focused their efforts on searching for the bodies.

My mother listens, weeping steadily beside me.

It's only been a few months since she emerged from a depression that hit her pretty hard. After her mother's death and her own retirement, she moved slowly but surely into a period of great anxiety. Everything around her changed completely. As if stepping into the lobby of this movie theater, she suddenly found herself confronted by a range of possibilities she had never dealt with before: 2-D dubbed versions, 2-D subtitled versions, 3-D dubbed versions, 3-D original-language versions, 4-DX dubbed and subtitled versions. So many new titles, so many movies, and there she was standing at the ticket booth, vulnerable to the whirlwind of stimuli. Who she was and how she had gotten to this point hardly mattered. The logic of cause and effect had broken down. The previous chapter was closed and everything that constituted her past was obsolete in the sea of perspectives opening before her. Then, without a prior plan to guide her choices, without the kind of solid script that takes years to write, with no gravitational force to make sense of her options, my mother, light and fragile, shot out into space. She was lost the way memories are lost. And there she drifted tethered by a flimsy cord, as we tried to toss her a cable to earth to restore her weight and gravity. My mother checked into that unnerving territory where 80 percent of my fellow citizens live. A brisk, upsetting place, ruled by psychiatrists, antidepressants, anti-anxiety drugs, and sleeping pills.

Now, as I listen to her cry, I realize it was a bad idea to ask her to come. A few weeks ago she adjusted her dose of Sentidol. Instead of three pills a day, she now takes two. She also announced, against the psychiatrist's orders, that she's done taking lorazepam to help her sleep, because at seventy-six she doesn't want to become a drug addict—that's what she said. She doesn't sleep anymore, or just a few hours here and there, so she's shaky and on edge, scratching at her head and hands all day until she breaks the skin, but fortunately safe from the threat of drug addiction. Considering her con-valescent state, I should have brought her to see a cheerier movie. I've worked on these images so much that I've grown used to them, lost all sensitivity to their effects, like a vul-ture. The revelatory shudder I felt when I first encountered them turned into something routine. Here are those pictures of the Lonquén kilns again. I see the skulls lined up neatly after the exhumation. I see the family members praying and crying with photographs of their loved ones pinned to their chests. I see these things, and what I think is that some pic-tures are missing. My robot brain analyzes, adds, and sub-tracts, reconstructing the Lonquén file from my computer, selecting and rejecting scenes and photographs that were reworked and deciding that some of the most effective, eloquent shots were omitted from this final cut.

But my mother next to me doesn't need more eloquence. She isn't a machine, and what's on the screen is more than enough for her. Her memory is fragile, so she's been sheltered. That's why she can't help crying as she watches, as if she's learning about it all for the first time. The hint of the past triggers her emotions and everything becomes present. Lonquén is here, unfolding before her eyes almost forty years later. In these frenetic and fractured times in which memories fall away, my mother can watch the same movie a thousand times and be as moved as if it's the first time.

In this lonely theater, my mother is part Barbara Jean Trenton, too, I think.

Everything she's seeing right now belongs to her past. The projected images revive a time that is more hers than mine, but she's done her healthy best to forget it, whereas I've inherited it as an unhealthy obsession.

The man talking about mass graves is a lawyer. I know him well because he's part of the chorus of voices I've been listening to over and over again lately. He's slightly younger than my mother; probably in his sixties. He speaks clearly, and, unlike the other subjects, he sometimes shows emotion when he recalls events in which he took part. The kilns and the dead at Lonquén are behind us now, and he is explaining on camera what his job at the Vicariate was. He says that he was the head of the Detained-Disappeared Unit. His brief was the dead. His aim: to track them and hunt for their bodies no matter where they might be. His search took him all over Chile. They called him the Hound because he followed the scent of blood.

Now he's talking about two informers who helped him in his task.

About one in particular.

One who was an active member of the intelligence services when he came forward to give his testimony.

The lawyer tells how this man was contacted through a magazine that the man had approached, desperate to make his statement. I want to talk, the lawyer says he said. The lawyer tells how, after reading what this man described to the reporter, he agreed to meet with him and interview him. Then came that August afternoon in the Plaza Santa Ana and the beginning of a relationship that I've been trying to imagine.

My cell phone screen lights up. There's a WhatsApp message for me. It's from my friends, the directors of the movie we're watching. I'd told them that I was planning to come, and now they're messaging, curious to know how many people are in the audience. I look around at the legion of red seats, all empty. From the theater above us comes a deafening sound, like an explosion. The walls and the floor vibrate slightly. Ultron must be battling the Avengers, probably in the middle of the climactic scene, the one that makes everybody shrink in their seats, popcorn hopping where it probably lies scattered on the floor by now. Meanwhile, my mother—the only first-time spectator in this theater—cries softly as on screen the lawyer addresses the camera. I keep thinking that there are images missing from the documentary, other shots that would've been more powerful, more earth-shaking. Maybe we should have reconstructed some scenes: brutal fights, hand-to-hand combat with evil agents. Maybe we should have hired stars like Robert Downey Jr. or, more realistically, a face familiar from the afternoon soaps. Maybe we should have included some special effects, or at least photoshopped wrinkles and gray hair, patched in a swelling sound track for each segment, and added something as spectacular and hair-raising as the explosion up above us that I can still hear. It's lunchtime, and the documentary I'm watching is an odd fit for a multiplex like this, so it makes some sense that my mother and I are the only ones here, but even so I can't bring myself to answer my friends' question. I'm afraid to confess that the one real audience member came because I brought her and she might only be crying because she's cut her dose of Sentidol. I write truthfully that I'm here with my mother and she's very moved. Then I tell them that I'll be in touch when the show is over and I turn off my phone.

On screen the lawyer is still talking. He says that the first thing he did with the man who tortured people was go in the Renault van to some of the places where the detained and disappeared had been buried. The lawyer says that the man who tortured people paced each spot, trying to remember; he counted his steps, did sums in his head, raked the soil with feet and hands. As I imagine it, at least, it strikes me as a moving scene. A man trying to summon his worst memories, meticulously attempting to mentally declassify their darkest details.

The lawyer says they also went to see some detention facilities. They sat outside peering in, hidden in the car as the man who tortured people described what he'd seen. The lawyer says it was a long afternoon of looking and searching. The lawyer says that after this excursion they arrived at a predetermined location, property of the Catholic Church, where they were expected. Once they got there, they asked expressly not to be disturbed. The lawyer says that they settled in, he took out a tape recorder, and they got to work. The lawyer says—and meanwhile I'm setting the scene and imagining it all, because I know his words so well I could repeat them by heart, even imitating the timbre of his voice:

Look, I'm going to record this, but I care less about the recording than your words. I want you to talk to me, and as you do I'm going to write. To me, writing means getting your words down. To me, writing means hearing and understanding what you're saying and what I should ask.

The lawyer says that after this explanation he started the tape recorder, that the tape spun in the machine, capturing the voice of the man remembering, in spare, precise sentences, without adjectives.

Thirty years after this encounter, on the screen here in the theater, the lawyer inserts an old cassette into a tape recorder. It's ancient, the kind that isn't used anymore. He carefully pushes Play, the tape inside turns, and from the machine's small, staticky speakers comes a man's voice.

It's him. What I hear over the theater speakers is the voice of Andrés Antonio Valenzuela Morales, Soldier First Class, ID #39432, La Ligua. His words, unfiltered by time or faulty memory. Testifying right there, a few hours after his suicidal despair, with the smell of death on him, still trying to get it off his body.

Each time I saw this image in previous cuts, I instinctively leaned toward whatever screen was in front of me to hear better. Now the theater's Dolby Surround Sound lets me listen without having to move from my red seat. As the lawyer listens to the testimony he gathered decades ago, the voice of the man who tortured people, trapped in the continuous present turning in the cassette tape, makes its way across the theater to me. For the first time, I hear it clearly. His words truly are spare, nouns unadorned by adjectives, sticking to what's strictly necessary. He mentions some agents, victims, one operative especially whose name I don't recognize. Little Fanta, Big Fanta, he says. He reels off memories, trying to identify prisoners, pinpointing facts, names, dates.

> *I didn't know I'd end up doing this.*
> *If I had known,*
> *I would've kept those IDs it was my job to destroy.*
> *Now we'd know who we're talking about.*
> *I can't remember their names. I remember nicknames.*
> *We called one guy the Watchmaker. One was the Vicar.*
> *One was Comrade Yuri.*

To me, writing means getting the words down. To me, writing means understanding what you're telling me, the lawyer said a little while ago, from the movie theater's screen. And before that, he said it from my computer screen as I watched.

And before that, he said it in front of my friends and their camera when they interviewed him. And before that, he actually said it in front of the man who tortured people, years ago, when he took his statement. And he'll keep saying it each time the film is shown, whenever anybody anywhere— even a single viewer—wants to see it. The camera captures the words of the man who tortured people, like the notes the lawyer took long ago and like the lines you are reading here. Captures them so the message won't be erased, so that what we don't yet understand can be deciphered by someone in the future. Captures them in order to anchor them to the earth, adding weight and gravity, so that nothing goes shooting into space and is lost.

This empty theater is a parenthesis in time, a spatiotemporal capsule, a spaceship in which my mother and I travel at a pace set by a clock telling a different time, the same as the one marking the hours at Barbara Jean Trenton's mansion in *The Twilight Zone*. One day her faithful agent comes to visit and she isn't in the living room. The bottle of whiskey is on its side on the floor and the projector is on, spinning one of the old reels she always used to watch. The agent glances at the movie playing on the screen. In it, everything is the same as always—same lines, same actions, same images— though with a single creepy difference. Barbara has crossed the threshold of the known, entering a dimension as vast as space and as timeless as infinity. Halfway between light and shadow, between science and superstition. Barbara Jean Trenton no longer inhabits time as we know it. She has immersed herself in the past, and from the screen she smiles at her faithful friend, bidding him farewell. Her smile is captured in celluloid, an indelible trace.

The theater vibrates with another explosion from *Avengers 2*. Out of the corner of my eye, I see my mother watching the images, moved, not registering the racket from above, probably because she's deaf in one ear. In the film, the lawyer stops the cassette and the voice of the man who tortured people can no longer be heard. It doesn't matter, I'll capture it here. Next come the sequences I know so well, anchoring me to this red seat like a safety belt. Again the bombing of La Moneda. Again the proclamations and the National Stadium and the detainees.

I'm a lonely actress past her prime, drinking whiskey all day long and trying to decipher ancient images that repeat over and over again.

My mind is back at Nido 18.
And Nido 20. And Remo Cero.
Also Colina and the spiral staircase at AGA that led to the
lower level.
I had never seen one.
Before we went down they lined us up.
They told us we had to forget everything we were about to see.
Wipe it from our minds.
Whoever remembered was a dead man.

I liked the sea.
I wanted to be a sailor, so I could go to sea.
But instead I joined the air force.
At first I was at the Colina base. I wasn't there for long.
Then they sent me to AGA, the Air War Academy,
to guard prisoners of war.
That's what they called them: prisoners of war.
When we got there they made us line up.
We went down that pipe-filled spiral staircase to the lower level.
It was like a submarine, I thought.
Many people were standing there.
They were blindfolded and handcuffed.
Others, the most valuable prisoners, were in the hallway.
There were signs on their backs.
"No food or water." "48 hours no sitting."

I had never been without food or water.
Had never stood for so long.
In my few months of military service
I had never experienced anything like that.

On the first night an alarm sounded.
Everything went dark.
Fifty machine guns had been
placed in strategic spots.
From the same direction, floodlights came on.
The light was dazzling. My eyes stung.

In such a situation we'd been instructed
to make all the prisoners lie down on the floor
with their hands behind their heads.
Even the ones with signs that said "48 hours no sitting."
If the officer gave the order
we were supposed to shoot and kill the detainees.

I had never killed anyone.

The officer on duty walked by with a grenade in his hand.
He was looking at us, not the prisoners.
He released the safety on the grenade and said that if we were
thinking about rescuing or helping any of the prisoners we'd
better forget it.
That if anybody made a move he would throw the grenade in
the hallway.
That if anybody made a move every damn fool in the room
would die.

I was stuck there for six months.
Then they took me to the houses.
Nido 18. Nido 20. Remo Cero.
I was nineteen years old.

There were three Flores brothers. Or at least there were three who got arrested. Boris Flores, Lincoyán Flores, and Carol Flores. The story of their detention is so similar to the others I've already imagined that at this point they all blur and run together in a montage, predictable and even a little dull.

It's noon and young Boris is at the door when he sees four cars and a police van turn slowly down his street. A national police officer with a hood pulled over his face leans out of the first car, pointing to the house. Young Boris knows what's coming, and he's terrified. He darts nervously inside, hoping to escape, but any attempt to hide is pointless, because from now on what follows is the unspooling of images already witnessed and recorded here before. Men with mustaches getting out of cars, men in civilian garb breaking down the door, moving through the house, overturning the furniture, finding Boris and seizing him and beating him and kicking him on the floor. And his mother screaming and his niece crying. And the neighbors pretending not to notice and hiding, not seeing or not wanting to see.

And then the other two brothers appear. Carol and Lincoyán. They've heard the commotion from somewhere and they come running in alarm. As one might imagine, they too are seized and beaten. And nothing does any good: not their mother's pleas, not their niece's tears, not the Floreses' resistance. As one might imagine, the commandos take the three brothers from their mother's house to some unspecified location.

The man who tortured people played no part in this arrest. Ten years later, he's at a parish hall. It's one of those places used for meetings or community events, but now it's empty, at the disposal of the man who tortured people and the lawyer working with him. They sit under a bare bulb. There are two cups of tea or coffee steaming on the table, poured a moment ago by some discreet nun who asked no questions and saw no more than she needed to see. There's also an ashtray holding a few cigarette butts, evidence that the two men arrived a while ago.

I imagine them facing each other, eyes meeting. The gaze of the man who tortured people sometimes drifts to the tape spinning and spinning in the lawyer's cassette recorder. I imagine the table is full of photographs. The man who tortured people examines them and tries to identify faces. He doesn't remember names; he remembers nicknames. This is the one we called the Vicar, this is the Watchmaker, this is Comrade Yuri, he says. All of these photographs were provided by family members of the disappeared. The lawyer is trying to track them down, that's his job, that's why he's brought the pictures, and that's why he's challenging the man who tortured people to remember them.

Each of these photographs is a postcard sent from some other time.

A cry for help begging to be heard.

The man who tortured people studies the photographs, trying to decipher what they're hiding. Territories inhabited by other people's lives and other people's pasts. Countries bounded by personal histories, regulated by laws invented at family dinner tables. The Contreras Maluje world, the Weibel world, the Flores world. Planets from which the only message to be heard is transmitted by smiling faces looking into the camera and begging to be recognized.

Remember who I am, they say.

Remember where I was, remember what was done to me. Where I was killed, where I was buried.

The man who tortured people holds one of these photographs in his hand. He examines it carefully. It shows a young man with a child in his arms. The man is looking into the camera and smiling shyly, while the child, barely a year old, looks faintly surprised. On the planet they're from, the child is most likely the son of the man who's holding him. The boy is wearing little white shoes and socks, maybe bought for him by his mother, who isn't visible, but who is part of the world that speaks through the photograph.

I imagine the man who tortured people is imagining this world. I imagine that, like me, he's able to read the moment when the photograph was taken. He can see the house, the family all around, and as he does so, I imagine, a faint shiver runs through him.

Remember who I am, he hears.

Remember where I was, remember what was done to me. Where I was killed, where I was buried.

The man who tortured people says that his job in the basement of the War Academy was to sit outside the rooms of detainees, rifle in hand, and make sure that no one spoke. The first room he was assigned was number two. In it was Carol Flores, the man in the photograph he's holding in his hand.

We called him Juanca, but his name was Carol, he says.

The Flores brothers were tortured at the War Academy. As Carol was being interrogated, young Boris heard his screams. In turn, Carol heard Lincoyán's screams. In turn, Lincoyán heard Boris's screams.

One day the youngest of the Flores brothers was taken out of the room where he was held and driven away in a truck. Young Boris made the trip on the floor, lying at the feet of his captors, who announced that they were going to kill him. Young Boris imagined a shot in the back of the head or a burst of machine gun fire behind him as he ran through some open field. He thought about his brothers Carol and Lincoyán, heard their screams of pain from the interrogation room again. And maybe he thought about his mother and his niece weeping, which was the last thing he heard before he was arrested. Maybe he thought about his father, or his other brother Fabio, or his girlfriend, because he must have had a girlfriend. But any last thoughts going through his head were interrupted by the sudden braking of the truck.

The doors flew open. He was blindfolded, and couldn't see as he advanced, but he soon realized that he was back at the Air War Academy. Back in the interrogation room. When they removed the blindfold, he realized that he wasn't in a field with some conscript's rifle pointed at the back of his head. They weren't going to kill him. They had never planned to. The drive he'd returned from was a kind of warning, that's how he understood it. But before he could reflect more on what he had been through, a man announced that he had to sign a statement and then he would be released. Boris agreed, and hours later, after being given a good beating, as one might imagine, he was dumped in the center of Santiago. Young Boris could hardly fathom what was happening but as soon as he recovered from the shock, he got on a bus and made it to the door of his brother Fabio's house, collapsing when someone answered his knock.

My son is fourteen. A little while ago he started taking the bus on his own. It's an ordinary thing now, but I don't like him to travel at night or to unfamiliar places. He's respectful of my fears: he's careful and calls and lets me know where he is, and he hasn't rebelled yet against my controlling ways. Boris Flores was three years older than my son and he crossed the city by bus, probably at night, hurting and broken after a month of being locked up. I can't imagine what his mother felt when she saw the men come for him. I can't even approach what went through her mind when she had to watch him being beaten and taken away. I don't know how she was able to bear that entire month with no news, searching for him and imagining him. I don't know how she must have reacted when she heard that he was back, when she saw him walk through the door and she was able to hug that seventeen-year-old body, battered by electric shocks and torture.

When young Boris arrived he was surprised to see his brother Lincoyán back home. In turn, Lincoyán was surprised to see Boris back home. And the two of them together in their turn were surprised when their brother Carol didn't return.

The man who tortured people says he kept guarding the prisoners. He learned to take them to their torture sessions. He learned to bring them back. He learned to keep watch so that they didn't talk among themselves; he learned to make them eat and prevent them from sitting down, if that was what was required. He learned well, and after a while, he was selected to be part of the reaction groups, as they were called. He was taken on operations, directing traffic while the others seized and arrested people.

At the same time, in the basement setting of the War Academy, I imagine Carol Flores still locked up in room number two. From within the confines of those four walls, he imagined his brothers at his mother's house, the place where they had been arrested and where they were surely now wondering what had become of him. An extra bowl of soup was served and grew cold daily on the Floreses' table. A seat was left empty for him every lunchtime, every dinnertime.

The man who tortured people says that one day he didn't see Carol Flores in room number two. He hadn't been taken to the interrogation room and he wasn't in the bathroom or anywhere else. The prisoners had gradually been leaving the lower levels of the AGA for other detention centers, so the man who tortured people guessed that Carol Flores had also been relocated.

Young Boris smiled happily when his brother Carol showed up at home. In turn, so did Lincoyán. And in their turn, so did their brother Fabio and their parents and Carol's wife and even his newborn son when they saw Carol back at home.

That day Carol Flores sat down at the table to eat his bowl of soup but he did not smile. He ate slowly as everyone watched. He lifted his spoon to his mouth robotically. Young Boris had a question for him, and Lincoyán shushed him. Young Boris had another question, and then his brother Fabio shushed him. Young Boris kept asking, and then his parents and his sister-in-law shushed him. And thus the third of the Flores brothers said absolutely nothing during dinner. He didn't talk about his three months in detention, he didn't talk about what had happened to him there, or how or why he'd been let go. He said hardly a thing when he saw his son for the first time. For a moment, the Floreses wondered whether this man sitting at the table with them was the same person who'd been taken away three months ago.

Carol Flores didn't look for work. He stayed home, smoking, sitting in an armchair, probably watching television. His wife cared for their newborn son, and watched this strange man who'd been returned to her. She remembered the other man, the one she had married, a restless young man full of energy, a man who had taken part in land grabs, a man who had enthusiastically joined militant factions in the party and at work. An extroverted, loving man, so very different from this silent man in the armchair.

After yet another day of television, cigarettes, and diapers, Carol's wife looked out the window and saw an alarming sight. In the street, standing by a car, was one of the men who had been there when the Floreses were arrested. Carol's wife screamed, terrified. She feared the worst. That they would take Carol again, that they would beat him to death. That they would take her, that she would be beaten to death. That her son would be left alone crying in an empty house. But no such thing happened. When he heard her scream, Carol came to the window and in a voice she had never heard before, he said: It's okay, it's just El Pelao Lito. Carol Flores went out to meet the man who was waiting for him. From then on, the man became his shadow.

A little while ago I saw a documentary by the French film-maker Chris Marker. It describes an episode during World War II that I had never heard of: the mass suicides in Okinawa. In 1945, the Allies invaded the island, which was of strategic importance in bringing about the final surrender of Japan. I don't know all the details of the battle, but what moved me most and what I'd like to tell is the testimony of one old man, a survivor who described his experiences to the camera.

Shigeaki Kinjo was in his twenties when it happened. Kinjo says that when the Allies' landing was imminent, Japanese soldiers deployed around the island handed out grenades to the guerrilla forces and civilians. Their instructions were clear: never surrender to the enemy. When the Allies arrived, the Japanese of Okinawa were to use the grenades to kill themselves. It didn't matter whether you were a soldier or a civilian, a man or a woman, a child or an old person, your destiny was to die. Those were the emperor's orders.

I suppose the Japanese army knew they would be defeated. Otherwise I can't explain this drastic decision. When the day came and Allied ships began to be glimpsed from the coasts, the people of Okinawa watched intently, well aware of what they had to do. Perhaps some thought about disobeying the emperor's orders and turning themselves over to the Allies, but they had been warned that the enemy were cruel devils who would behead them, rape their women, burn down their houses, and crush their bodies with tanks.

When the moment came to commit suicide, the grenades didn't work. Or at least not for the civilian population, who had never used grenades before. Bewildered, frantic, afraid, the people of Okinawa didn't know what to do. The enemy was upon them and they had no way to save their families, their wives, their daughters, their elderly parents, no way to grant them the saving grace of death. Kinjo describes how he watched one of his desperate neighbors take up heavy tree branches and beat his wife and children. The man wept as he did so, but he was convinced that it was an act of salvation. The screams of his family did nothing to soften the harsh blows. Each stroke was followed by an even more brutal one. One, two, twenty, thirty blows. Or maybe more, until his wife and children lay dead on the ground.

A dark silence fell over that corner of the island.

All who had witnessed the scene were left stunned and speechless.

For a moment the collective hysteria was stilled by the sight of the bloodied bodies.

Young Kinjo was there, neither man nor child. He stared in fear. Maybe he heard a flock of birds cross the sky. Maybe he heard the sound of the waves in the distance, crashing against some cliff. Or maybe somebody screamed again, reactivating minds and bodies, and then it was the beginning of the end. Without much thought, Kinjo and other desperate Japanese took other big branches from other big trees and with them they began to beat the other wives, the other sisters, the other elders. Kinjo struck his mother on the head. Then he struck his younger siblings. He wept as he did so, or so he said on camera, but he was convinced that it was an act of salvation. His family's cries did nothing to soften the harsh blows. Each stroke was followed by an even more brutal one. One, two, twenty, thirty. Or maybe more, until his mother and his siblings were dead, bloody and broken, along with the rest of that big island family of Okinawa.

Japanese history tried to erase the episode from its textbooks.
Japanese history tried to erase the episode from its past.

Young Kinjo, who is now an old man, tried to kill himself after he had killed his family, but he couldn't do it. Now he's ashamed when he speaks on camera. He says he acted against nature, thinking that he was in the right, that he was doing something heroic by following the emperor's orders. His actions were as cruel as an enemy's would have been. And in fact, young Kinjo, who is an old man now, says that without realizing it he turned into his worst enemy.

I think about Carol Flores and the strange closeness he developed with the man who arrested him: El Pelao Lito. I think about the fine line he crossed in order to draw near to his adversary, to invite him into his home, to no longer fear El Pelao Lito when his captor came in search of him.

When young Boris heard about this relationship, he asked his brother Carol about it, but Carol didn't answer. When Lincoyán heard about it, he asked too. And so did Fabio and their parents, but Carol never answered.

The man who tortured people says that he knew El Pelao Lito well. His real name was Guillermo Bratti, a fellow air force soldier. He came from El Bosque Air Base and also passed through the Air War Academy. Later they crossed paths at Cerrillos Air Base, where they were transferred, and they began to work together in the same antisubversive shock group. Everybody was there: El Chirola, El Lalo, El Fifo, El Yerko, El Lutti, El Patán. Their objective was to break up the Communist Party and that was why El Pelao Lito was selected to work with a party informer. That informer was Carol Flores, alias El Juanca.

Each day, Carol Flores, or El Juanca, began to do what the man who tortured people is doing right now. El Pelao Lito would pick Carol up and drive him to the office to sort through information. Carol Flores, or El Juanca, sat at a table like the one in this parish hall, interpreting statements gathered in the interrogations of detainees. He, too, was confronted with a thousand photographed faces and he, too, had to identify them. This is Arsenio Lea; this is Miguel Ángel Rodríguez Gallardo, El Quila Leo; this is Francisco Manzor; this is Alonso Gahona, I imagine he said. The man who tortured people says that Carol Flores, or El Juanca, became one of them. He carried his own gun and he started to participate in the detentions and interrogations of his former comrades.

Did young Boris know this? Did Lincoyán? Did Fabio?

One day Carol's father received a visit from his son. Carol asked his father to come outside with him to talk. He didn't want anyone to overhear them. Then, for the first time, Carol told his father what had happened to him when he was detained. He talked to him about the lower levels at AGA, the interrogations, the torture sessions, young Boris's screams, his brother Lincoyán's screams. He told him about the final pact that he had decided to sign with his enemies. He would collaborate with them if they let his brothers go, releasing them from any possibility of detention. And that was what happened. The Floreses were freed from danger in exchange for Carol's soul. Carol was convinced that this was an act of salvation.

Did young Boris know this? Did Lincoyán? Did Fabio?

For the first time in a long time, Carol's father recognized the son he once had. In those despairing eyes he recognized his son's gaze. In those sad words he recognized his son's voice. Everything that had remained hidden in the man returned from detention now surfaced. At last Carol was back, but only to say a final goodbye and be replaced, once and for all, by the fearsome Juanca.

The photograph that the man who tortured people is looking at is from that exact time, I imagine. Carol's son is a few months old and he's in his father's arms, wearing those little white shoes. Carol is part Carol and part El Juanca in this shot. His smile is strange, uncomfortable, remote. The man who tortured people knows that expression. He recognizes it, because it's tattooed on his own face.

Remember who I am, he hears from the photograph.
   Remember where I was, remember what they did to me.

Carol Flores, or El Juanca, sometimes went to El Pelao Lito's house for lunch. The two of them sat in armchairs, staring into space, as the children played over their outstretched legs. They ate bean stew, they smoked, they watched television, and they went out again on some covert operation. Each time they returned they seemed thinner, more tired, more broken down, more taciturn, more silent. This happened over and over again until one day they didn't come back.

Young Boris never saw his brother Carol again. Neither did Lincoyán. Neither did Fabio, or their parents, or his wife, or the children. The Floreses left an empty chair at lunch and dinner. The soup grew cold once and for all.

The man who tortured people never saw Carol Flores or El Juanca again either.

The man who tortured people says that one night he and his fellow agents were brought in for a special operation. They were driven to a detention center, where his superiors were waiting for them in the midst of a cocktail party. There was pisco and pills and everybody drank and ate. When the drinks were finished they called in the "package"—that was the word they used, he said. The package was El Pelao Lito, handcuffed and blindfolded. He made a mistake, they were told, he was a traitor, you don't play around with information, whose side was he on. The man who tortured people says he didn't know what was happening, but he gathered that El Pelao Lito had done something bad, had betrayed the group by revealing some secret. That was why they forced him kicking and screaming into the trunk of a car and took him to the Cajón del Maipo. There, in the middle of the mountain night, they let him out and they shot him, just as he had done to so many of his own targets. Just as had been done to José Weibel, to Carlos Contreras Maluje. The man who tortured people says that he had to bind El Pelao Lito's hands and feet and throw him into the river. The man who tortured people says that he was scared. For a moment it crossed his mind that the same thing could befall him some day. El Pelao Lito was his comrade, he was twenty-five years old. The man who tortured people had never imagined having to witness the death of one of his own at the hands of their group. He had never imagined what a fine line it was that separated his comrades from his enemies.

The man who tortured people says that a little while later he learned that Carol Flores, or El Juanca, had suffered the same fate. His body turned up in the river riddled with seventeen bullet holes, his fingers severed at the first joint, his spinal column snapped, and his genitals exploded.

The Floreses saw the photograph of the body many years after the man who tortured people gave his testimony. In the photograph, the Floreses recognized a son, a brother, a husband. It was him. Carol, not Juanca. He was missing his teeth, his forehead was beaten out of shape, but it was the Carol Flores they had always loved and looked for. Not the enemy, not the informant.

I remember another episode from *The Twilight Zone*. In it a man could choose a new face whenever he needed to. He was the so-called man of a thousand faces. He kept all of the faces inside, and depending on the context, he used whichever best fit the circumstances. If he had been on Okinawa he would have been a peaceful, happy neighbor until the war and then a savage murderer of his own family. If he had been in Chile in the seventies he would have been a happy municipal employee of La Cisterna or a young peasant from Papudo who dreamed of being a policeman or a sailor, and then a savage agent, willing to torture or turn in his loved ones.

How many faces can a human being contain?

What about young Boris? How many did he contain?

What about his brother Lincoyán?

What about the lawyer listening to the man who tortured people?

What about the man himself? What about me?

We crossed a bridge and the car turned left.
We drove down a dirt road.
We stopped after about seven kilometers,
approximately forty meters from the cliff.

It was cold.
I guess there was a moon because everything was clear.
They got El Pelao out of the trunk and took him to a rock
about ten meters away.
How do you want to die? they asked.
With no handcuffs and no blindfold, he said.

They ordered me to remove them.
I crept toward him.
I was a wreck. I could hardly look at him.
It's windy, Papudo, he said, it's a cold night.
And I couldn't answer him, the words wouldn't come out.

I was scared. Everybody but me was an officer.
I thought they were going to throw me down there with El Pelao.

I took off his handcuffs.
And they sent me for rope and wire.
I was in the car getting them when I heard the burst of gunfire.
It was cold.

I guess there was a moon because everything was clear.
When I got back, El Fifo Palma was finishing him off.
I didn't see anyone else shoot.

They ordered me to bind El Pelao's hands and feet.
They ordered me to tie stones to him.
They ordered me to push him off the cliff.

I remembered the last time we had lunch together.
It hadn't been so long ago.
We'd talked about soccer.
We'd told jokes.

Because of all the bushes
I had to hang over the edge myself.
Someone gripped my hand.
And I dangled there as I pushed El Pelao over.
I thought they would let me go too.
But no. He fell alone.
I guess there was a moon
because I saw him clearly down there in the river.
I can't get it out of my mind.
When we got back we drank a whole bottle of pisco.

On April 12, 1961, Major Yuri Gagarin became the first astronaut to travel to outer space. For one hundred and eight minutes he orbited Earth in his ship, the *Vostok 1*, and from up above he was able to take the measure of our planet with his own eyes. He saw that it was blue, round, and beautiful. That's what he said in his transmission to mission control: Earth is beautiful. My science teacher, the one with the big mustache I mentioned before, once got very excited telling us about the Soviet space program and Gagarin's amazing feat. I can't remember whether it was part of something we were studying or whether he just felt like telling us the story, but his enthusiasm was contagious and that's probably why I remember the class when he drew *Vostok 1* for us on the blackboard, which stood in for outer space. He didn't tell us about the little dog Laika, or about Valentina Tereshkova, the first woman in orbit, or about Neil Armstrong and his walk on the moon. My teacher talked only about Major Gagarin, as if his flight twenty years before had been the most important one, the definitive one.

After that class I realized a few things. One interesting discovery was that there were a number of Yuris floating around my neighborhood and my life. I knew it was a Soviet name, but I didn't know why it was popular in Chile. I had never met a Nikolai or an Anton or a Pavlov or a Sergei. In fact, I had never met anyone with a Soviet name, because at that time anything Soviet was definitely not popular. But I had met several Yuris.

Our mustached teacher told us how Major Gagarin became a star the moment he returned from his voyage. The government of the Soviet Union trotted him around the world as an ambassador, a public relations phenomenon. No one could be indifferent to the smile of the man who had seen what no one else had ever seen. So Major Gagarin was replicated all over the world. In Egypt, Cuba, Mexico, Chile, everybody wanted to be a little bit like him, and as an homage they called their children Yuri, a name that honored not only the cosmos but also a nation heralding itself as a present-day and future utopia. Yuri Pérez, Yuri Contreras, Yuri Soto, Yuri Bahamondes, Yuri Riquelme, Yuri Gahona. An army of South American cosmonauts were born in Chile as a tribute to Major Gagarin and his trip, the idea that Earth was blue and beautiful, and the conviction that in outer space no voice of a god could be heard.

I imagine Don Alonso Gahona Chávez, employee of the district of La Cisterna, looking into the face of his newborn son and speaking the name with which he'll be baptized. I imagine him years later, on a soccer field, playing ball with his son and shouting that same name when his son scores a goal. I imagine him sitting at a chessboard, trying to teach his son the game's basic moves. Pawns advance one space at a time, rooks in a straight line, and bishops on the diagonal. The queen attacks—and, most importantly, protects the king. I imagine him out for a walk in the country one night, looking up at the stars, and telling his son enthusiastically, as my teacher once told me, about the great feat of the man who saw the world from up above for the first time, long ago in 1961. About the voyage of that mythic cosmonaut, from whom, I venture to imagine, Don Alonso's young son inherited his name: Yuri Gahona.

I imagine that on September 8, 1975, when little Yuri was just seven years old, he began to set up the chessboard as he waited for his father to get home from work. I imagine him taking one of the white bishops and pretending the piece is a rocket ship. Little Major Gagarin, or Yuri Gahona, imagines that he's inside that bishop, flying over the chessboard, across each black and white square. From inside he gazes at the rest of the pieces down below as he carefully steers his plastic ship. Little Major Gagarin, or Yuri Gahona, imagines rising above the dining room table, above the stained rug; he imagines flying down the hall, through the whole house, until he reaches the front door, where he looks out to see whether his father is coming. I imagine little Major Gagarin, or Yuri Gahona, radar on, looking out from his miniature ship and informing ground control of what he sees. Or rather, what he doesn't see, because his father, who is the sole objective of his search, has yet to appear. He isn't walking down the street with his hands tucked into his jacket pockets, as always at this time of day. There's no sign of his slight figure, his coarse short hair, his thick glasses. Then little Major Gagarin, or Yuri Gahona, pretends to fly his bishop rocket ship even higher. He imagines that he reaches the roof of the house and that he climbs above the electric lines and up into the clouds and he looks out over the whole block, the whole neighborhood, the whole district, thus perhaps, with his Lilliputian cosmonaut's eye, detecting his father's exact location as he walks home.

Between Stop 25 and Stop 26 on Gran Avenida, on his daily walk home, Don Alonso Gahona Chávez has been ambushed by three armed men. One of them is Carol Flores, his former comrade, Communist Party member, close friend, and former fellow La Cisterna municipal employee. I imagine it's hard for Don Alonso to understand why his comrade is pointing a gun at him and ordering him to place his hands on the wall as the other two men pat him down. Quiet, Alonso, better not to make a scene, he hears him say. I imagine Don Alonso is confused, but he soon realizes what's going on and he gives himself up because he knows there's no way out. This is no assault, as some unsuspecting person might think. The people who see what's happening as they walk home, people out buying bread or getting on a bus, know perfectly well what's going on. And yet they give a sideways glance and keep going without saying or doing a thing, letting the armed men wrestle Don Alonso Gahona Chávez into a truck.

Little Major Gagarin, or Yuri Gahona, and his six-year-old sister, Evelyn, understand that if the chessboard was left untouched all night it's because something bad has happened to their dad. Probably it was Don Alonso himself who prepared them for an emergency like this. Just as he'd taught them how to move the chess pieces, maybe he also taught them how to act when the king has been snatched from the board. The children help search for Don Alonso, visiting army posts, police stations, hospitals, courthouses, even climbing trees and trying to look into a detention center to see if they can spot him. But it's no good. Not even by flying over the whole city in his white bishop spaceship can little Major Gagarin, or Yuri Gahona, find a trace of his father. No question about it, the bishop has failed to protect the king.

Let's open this door. Beyond it is the twilight zone. You're entering an unknown land of dreams and ideas. You're entering the twilight zone.

Nido 20. This was the name of one of the secret sites serving as detention centers in the district of La Cisterna, located at 037 Calle Santa Teresa. It got its name because it was run by Air Force Intelligence, and as an instition the air force seems to have a complete monopoly on anything having to do with birds, starting with the nest (*nido*) where they're born. The number 20 was chosen because of the site's location at Stop 20 on Gran Avenida.

I know—I'm not imagining—that Don Alonso Gahona was transferred to this place.

I know—I'm not imagining—that he crossed the threshold of 037 Calle Teresa and at that very moment he entered a dimension from which he would never return.

I search for information about the site and I discover that the house has been turned into a memorial. Former Nido 20 Memorial Site, House Museum of Human Rights Alberto Bachelet Martínez. That's what they call it. I write to an email address on the web page to ask about visiting hours, and a few hours later I'm sent a telephone number to schedule a meeting with the center's director. This takes me aback. I don't think

I need an appointment with the director of the memorial. I tend to believe that the directors of anything are busy people, and I just want to visit, see the place, compare what I see to what I know. Since I have no choice, I call the number I've been given. After a brief wait, the voice of an older man answers. He's in his seventies, I calculate, and he's the director of the memorial. I tell him I'd like to visit, but there are no hours listed on the web page. He replies kindly that in fact there are no visiting hours, but he'll expect me that afternoon. I explain that it isn't necessary for him to make special arrangements for me, I don't want to take up his time, but he tells me he's the only one who can let me in because there's no one else to oversee the place. The director doesn't need my name or any particular information for our appointment, he just calls me comrade and tells me he'll expect me at 5:00.

When I arrive, the outside of the house surprises me. It's dingy, and the front yard is full of junk and debris. There's no bell and the lock on the front gate is broken. A chain wrapped in thick blue plastic is looped uselessly around the two sides of the gate. Inside the gate, a broken-down taxi is parked off to one side. It's a small, single-story house with a stone chimney, a gate for cars, a red-tiled roof, and a big yard where there was once a pool. With some repairs it could be a snug home. I might have chosen it for my own family. Great transportation, shopping nearby, all the requirements for a peaceful, happy life. Another thing that surprises me is that it's in the middle of a residential neighborhood and less than ten meters from Gran Avenida, a major thoroughfare, full of cars and people at all hours. Forty years have passed since this house was a clandestine detention center, but I know that Gran Avenida was just as busy back then. It's still a commercial street and a public transit artery. The houses in the area resemble each other, surely part of some planned development from the sixties. On the corner are a couple of small shops. Some cars are parked on the street, and, a few meters away, a boy is shooting goals on the sidewalk. How much must these surroundings have changed over the years? I wonder. The answer is very little. Few things can be different than they were in 1975.

But I'm one of them.

The boy with the ball is another.

From my present, which was once Don Alonso Gahona's future, I imagine the truck in which he was abducted. I see it speeding past buses and cars along Gran Avenida itself, that September afternoon in 1975. It reaches Stop 20 and turns onto Calle Santa Teresa, pulling up here in front of the house, the same spot where I am now.

I imagine Don Alonso Gahona getting out of the truck.

Maybe Carol Flores is with him. Maybe he isn't.

I imagine Don Alonso Gahona being pushed through this same gate I'm standing in front of. He doesn't see me, of course. Actually, he doesn't see anyone from beneath the blindfold covering his eyes. He just obeys and lets himself be led by his captors. He walks with difficulty. I imagine him stumbling over the two steps that I can see from here, at the front door, as the neighbors watch, too. Then I think I see a woman spying from the house across the street. She peers out, hiding behind the curtain. Or maybe she's not hiding, and instead she stares openly as she waters the plants in her front yard. I imagine her and others like her watching the activity at this place day after day, as surprise turns into familiarity. The cries from torture sessions coexisting with the music on neighborhood radios, dialogue from the 3:00 p.m. soaps, the announcer's voice on the broadcast of the soccer match. The prisoners going in and out of this gate became part of the landscape. Like the mailman, the municipal inspector, the children walking to school early in the morning. Hearing the occasional gunshot wasn't strange anymore, it was part of the new sounds, the new habits, part of the daily routine that established itself emphatically, with no one daring to protest.

Little Major Gagarin, or Yuri Gahona, and his sister, Evelyn, never saw the scene that I've just imagined. They lived in the same district, but they didn't know anything about Nido 20. Despite how near it was, no one told them what was happening here. They never came to look through the bars in hopes of spotting their father, never flew over the block in their imagination, scanning for him from up above in their white bishop spaceship. Like me, they never saw what was happening inside this house. To get inside and imagine what went on here, the only person who can help us is the man who tortured people: Andrés Antonio Valenzuela Morales, Soldier First Class, ID #39432, La Ligua.

The man who tortured people says that after he worked guarding political prisoners at the Air War Academy and a hangar at Cerrillos Air Base, he was transferred to Nido 20 to do the same thing. The man who tortured people says that his job there was to watch the detainees, take them to their torture sessions, bring them food, make sure they didn't talk to each other. He says there were so many of them they had to expand into other detention centers. The man who tortured people says that at Nido 20 they had as many as forty prisoners at once. The man who tortured people says they had to use the closet for solitary confinement because there wasn't room anywhere else.

Of course, he doesn't say any of this to me.
   I keep mixing up my tenses.

Present, future, and past mingle on this street in a time bracketed by the twilight zone stopwatch. Sitting in the front seat of the Renault van, that's where I imagine him, outside the house with the lawyer. They watch the place surreptitiously from a distance, as they know how to do, without raising suspicions. They've gone on a long drive, visiting the places that the man described to the reporter. Cuesta Barriga, La Firma, the Cerrillos hangar, and now Nido 20. The lawyer wishes he had a camera, but instead he scrutinizes every detail, trying to memorize all he sees, just as I'm doing now. The man who tortured people is describing what he remembers about this house, and among his memories, he says that one of the prisoners who spent time there was Don Alonso Gahona. He says Don Alonso was known among his comrades by the nickname Yuri.

The first thing I see when I enter the house is a portrait of Don Alonso Gahona. It's an oil painting, framed and hanging next to the fireplace. It's a copy of the same photograph that I saw in the Museum of Memory. Alonso is smiling, wearing his thick glasses and bare-chested, because he's at the beach, I think. The director of the center greets me and tells me that this is Comrade Yuri. He doesn't say Alonso, he says: Yuri. Then he invites me in and asks me to sit down in what must once have been the living room. He asks me to wait a moment because he's meeting with a comrade, introducing her to me without mentioning her name. I expect I'll be ushered into some office or waiting room, but no. Suddenly I'm in the middle of a meeting, the main subject of which is the arrival of gypsies in the neighborhood. The comrade is very upset because she was fined by an inspector of the district of La Cisterna for an addition that she's building on her house, which is nearby, in the same development. But no one has said anything to her neighbor, one of the gypsies who've moved into the neighborhood, about the construction of a bay window overlooking her yard, which according to her is completely unauthorized and illegal. The comrade is sure the municipal inspectors have been bought off by the gypsies. That's the only way she can understand why they're never fined or made to pay taxes. The director of the center accepts her complaint and tells the neighbor he'll bring it to the comrade councilwoman and the comrade mayor himself. The director of the center has his own complaint to file because people have been throwing dead rats onto the grounds of the Former Nido 20 Memorial and they've put glue in the front lock, which is why it's broken and they have to secure the gate with a chain, so he'll attach the comrade's complaint to his personal complaint. Surely the comrade councilwoman and the comrade mayor will attend to their requests. After a cordial farewell, the comrade exits the memorial with the director, and I'm left alone in this house that was once a detention and torture center, with the photograph of Comrade Yuri staring at me from the mantelpiece.

The place is messy. Dust, lots of chairs scattered around the empty space, a sideboard full of old magazines, and a screen covered in colored paper. Displayed on it are photocopies of the faces of other prisoners with their names and nicknames written in black felt-tip marker. El Quila Leo, Comrade Díaz, Comrade Diego. All the sheets are stuck to the display with tape and risk coming unstuck. El Quila Leo looks at me a bit crookedly, listing to the right, about to fall to the floor. Everything is very precarious, handmade, like some kind of school report. Next to the painting of Comrade Yuri is one of Allende, another of Neruda, and finally one of General Bachelet, the president's father, after whom the memorial is named.

The comrade director comes back in and explains that as a human rights organization they offer services to the community. They act as a nexus between local residents and the mayor, and they also host biomagnetism sessions in the back room, offered by a therapist comrade for a modest fee. Right now the comrade is treating a Peruvian woman who has stomach cancer, he says. The comrade director tells me he's a taxi driver, which is why his taxi is parked in the house's front entrance. By night he drives the taxi and by day he runs the memorial. It isn't easy. There's no funding, and the Communist comrades aren't happy that he's in charge. All the prisoners who came through Nido 20 were Communists, so the party can't understand why a socialist comrade like him is the director of the memorial. It strikes them as inappropriate. They don't like him parking his

97

taxi here, either. After apologizing for the mess, the comrade director offers to show me the house.

The man who tortured people says that Don Alonso Gahona, Comrade Yuri, spent long sessions in the room where I am now. It was the designated location for torture. A small space, once a laundry room. The floor is red tiles with white grout, like the ones in my kitchen. There's a window that faces the street, directly across from another window in the house across the street. Taped to the walls are a couple of posters with drawings of different forms of torture. They're illustrations by the comrades who survived this room. On one I read *submarino*. Next to the handwritten word I see the drawing of a naked man with his head in a bucket of water or maybe urine. Two men are holding him down. From the drawing I understand that the intent was to cause the detainee to come close to drowning. On the poster next to it I read *piscina con hielo*. Here the drawing shows another man, naked and bound, in a tub full of ice. In the drawing, there are random letters around the man's body. They don't mean anything, they're just there as a kind of sign, a secret code that I don't understand and the comrade director can't explain. On the floor of the room is a little metal bed frame that might be a child's. The comrade director explains that in fact it is a child's cot. It was the only thing they could get to represent the frame that the torturers used for strapping down their prisoners and administering electric shocks.

The man who tortured people says this is what they did to Comrade Yuri. They strapped him to the *parrilla*, as they called those metal frames, and they beat him and shocked him. The man who tortured people says that after a long session they hung him in the shower of the bathroom that the comrade director is showing me now. It's a small bathroom, barely big enough for the two of us, tiled in blue and green with a quite tasteful sink and mirror, that's what I think when I walk in. Once upon a time somebody must have chosen them with care. Once upon a time somebody must have considered how nice they would look in their house's bathroom. Once upon a time somebody bought them and installed them and used them. Someone washed their hands in this sink. Someone brushed their hair and put on makeup in front of this mirror. And yet, the whole sixties-ish ensemble that goes so well with the tiles is the setting for this scene that the man who tortured people is remembering and describing.

Comrade Yuri was incredibly thirsty after the shocks he'd been given in the torture room. The man who tortured people says Comrade Yuri asked for water and one of the guards left the shower running so Comrade Yuri could drink. The man who tortured people says the guard turned the water off, but Comrade Yuri still complained of thirst. Weak as he was, he used the little strength he had to turn the water back on, but he wasn't able to drink, or to turn it off again. The man who tortured people says the water ran all night over Comrade Yuri's body. The man who tortured people says that by the next morning Comrade Yuri was dead, felled by a swift and deadly case of pneumonia.

I'm in the room where the prisoners slept on the floor. It's a small room, which must originally have been the bedroom where somebody laid their head and maybe had happy dreams

99

before embarking on their daily routine. From this bedroom over to the green-tiled bathroom, then on to breakfast in the living room where I heard talk about gypsies, and finally out the door and down those two steps over which Comrade Yuri stumbled a while later. As many as forty men shared this space, including those who were shut in the tiny closet in solitary confinement.

The comrade director shows me the mural they've made. It's a big painting of Comrade Yuri against a backdrop of bright colors that I don't know how to interpret. The mural is signed by the Red Star Brigade, and it's a project of Comrade Yuri's children, who have close ties to the memorial. The comrade director tells me he believes that since the body of Comrade Yuri was never found, the children—who are no longer children, because Yuri and Evelyn Gahona must be about my age or a little older—visit the memorial like a shrine or a tomb to remember their father. They've even requested that no work be done on the bathroom where Comrade Yuri died, that it remain untouched, says the comrade director. Green and small, just as it is now on my visit.

Once I saw photographs of Major Gagarin in his spaceship, the *Vostok 1*. Buckled into a tiny compartment, he traveled the cosmos in utter stillness. Only his eyes moved, and his hands, too, I think, as he gazed at Earth and the universe through a round window.

I imagine Comrade Yuri immobilized in that bathroom. With what little energy he has, he drinks the water falling on his naked body. There are no windows, but if he closes his eyes he can imagine a round window in the ceiling, just above his tired head. I imagine Comrade Yuri looking out that imaginary window. It's a starry night. The water is still falling on his body, but everything is so beautiful and blue out there that it's hard to concentrate on anything else. Suddenly, in the middle of the sky that's keeping him company, he thinks he sees a white blur. At first he supposes it's a falling star and he even has the old impulse to make a wish. But then he realizes that what he's seeing isn't a star, but something even more fascinating.

A chess piece crossing outer space.

A white bishop spaceship signaling to him from up above, attempting a rescue.

The man who tortured people says that the body of Don Alonso Gahona, Comrade Yuri, was wrapped in plastic and stuffed into the trunk of a car. The man who tortured people says he doesn't know where the body was taken, but he suspects it was dumped in the sea.

I imagine Comrade Yuri's body sinking somewhere along the Chilean coast. Maybe near the beaches of Papudo. Or maybe not. I imagine him descending into the depths of the blue sea that Major Gagarin saw from space, coloring the whole planet. Earth is blue, he said over the radio, looking out his round window at the sea in which years later Comrade Yuri would sleep forever. Earth is blue and beautiful, he said, and from where I sit let it go down in history, let it never be forgotten: there's no god to be heard.

In spite of myself I got deeper and deeper in.
Suddenly I wasn't the person I used to be.

I could blame my bosses.
I could say that they were the ones who changed me.
But you always have a hand in what happens to you.

I know this because I've seen people who don't betray
themselves.
People who might be up to their necks in shit and they don't
break.
El Quila Leo, for example.
That was one prisoner I came to admire.

His name was Miguel Rodríguez Gallardo.
He was a lathe operator, he had three little children.

He took a beating and he never talked.
They shocked him, they hit him, they hung him up, they
locked him away.
And he didn't talk.
El Quila found ways
to keep his mind clear, to keep it together.
El Quila listened carefully to sounds,
he took note of the smells, temperatures,

shapes, and colors he managed to observe
when he wasn't blindfolded.

I'm being held at Cerrillos Airport, he said to me one day.
How do you know? It could be Pudahuel
or El Bosque Air Base.
Every day I hear the instructions from the control tower
and they've never announced the takeoff of a fighter jet
or a passenger plane,
so it has to be Cerrillos, he said, and he was right.

When they brought him to Nido 20 he guessed where he was.
This is Stop 20 on Gran Avenida, he said.
The siren that goes off on the hour is from the firehouse where I
was a fireman.

El Quila knew when it was daytime.
El Quila knew when it was nighttime.
El Quila smelled flowers
and guessed the change of seasons.

When he was locked in the closet,
he looked for drawings on the wooden planks
and he made up stories about them,
he told them to himself.

He could tell us apart by the sound of our footsteps.
When we walked by, he called us by name
and he was always right.
He had his head on straight, much straighter than mine.

One night they called me.
They told me to put pikes, shovels, a few machine guns
and several liters of gasoline in a truck.
Then they gave us a list of detainees.
We had to bind and blindfold them.
One of them was El Quila.
He had been with us for more than four months.

They're going to let you go,
I lied as I covered his eyes with a blindfold.
Yes, he said. I'll be going free, but I'm not going home.

Before I tied him up he shook my hand
and held it for a moment.
I gave him a cigarette and he thanked me for it.

I started to cry as I was tying him up.
I cried silently, trying not to let him see,
but both of us knew what was going to happen.

El Quila went with the other detainees in the truck.
I kept his ID card.
Also his driver's license,
his watch, his wallet.
I had to make everything disappear.
I burned them and buried them, same as they did to him.

One day, a little while ago, I was with another agent in a car.
Someone had gotten run over.
The body was crushed

under the wheels of a bus.
*The other agent drove past very slowly, and I realized that he
liked looking.*
I couldn't look. I turned away.
I'm used to dead bodies.
I've seen lots of them by now,
but even so I couldn't look.
We were eating sandwiches.
The other agent kept eating. He finished his entire sandwich.

We had been innocent conscripts. Dumb. Naive.
*Now we were able to eat sandwiches while gawking at a dead
body.*

I thought about El Quila.
I thought about how much I cried when they killed him.
*I imagined him there, out in the open, before he was riddled
with bullets.*
*We're in Peldehue, he must have guessed from under the
blindfold.*
I cried slowly, secretly, so that no one would notice.
Some time later I felt grief, a knot in my throat.
Some time later I was able to control my tears.
Some time later I stopped crying.
Whether I wanted to or not, I had gotten used to it.
In the end I felt nothing.

I had become someone else.
Someone who gets up and goes to bed with the smell of death.

I don't want my children to know what I was, he says. I'm going back to my job and I'll pay the price for what I've done.

I don't care whether they kill me.

For three days the lawyer has been taking his testimony in the parish hall. I imagine that both men are weary and overwhelmed by all the probing.

I'm only doing this so there are no more deaths, says the lawyer. You're helping us with the truth, but not in exchange for your life. We won't do anything with your testimony until we get you to a safe place.

I imagine that a long time goes by.

I imagine that silence and cigarette smoke fill the room.

I imagine that they sip coffee. That some nun silently comes and goes.

I imagine that for a moment, maybe only a second, the man who tortured people sees himself inserted into one of those photographs still watching him from the table.

Remember who I am, they keep saying.

Remember where I was, remember what was done to me. Where they killed me, where they buried me.

It's a vast chorus. Smiling faces, bright eyes, all posing for the camera while on an outing or at some gathering or party, alongside family members, children, brothers or sisters, friends, in the happy past that everyone was once a part of. A distant and now nonexistent place, from which this man looking at the photographs was barred. He imagines himself as just another face among these lost people. He sees himself with his own children, his wife, maybe his parents, whom he hasn't visited for a while. He pretends they're on a beach in Papudo, sunning themselves and eating hard-boiled eggs, relaxing after a pickup soccer game and a nice dip in the sea, feet covered in black sand. They seem happy living a life that was never theirs. A life that he was never able to live because unwittingly he entered the dark parallel dimension where any photograph like this is part of an ancient reality or simply nonexistent.

You're right, he says. I won't go back to my job. I'm going to desert, with you as witness.

I imagine that the man who tortured people then reaches into his pocket. From an old wallet he removes his armed forces card, Andrés Antonio Valenzuela Morales, Soldier First Class, ID #39432 of La Ligua. In the center is a photograph numbered 66650, which I'm not imagining, which I have here in front of me, on a photocopied sheet that the lawyer himself gave me years later when we talked about this moment. In the photograph, the man who tortured people is posing for the camera in his uniform. His hair is neatly combed and he's clean-shaven, no mustache. Eyes wide. Three deep furrows in his brow, too deep for someone his age. On the lapel of his impeccable military uniform are two air force eagle pins.

The lawyer takes the card.

In the parish hall, the desertion is registered.

The face of the man who tortured people lies on the table, exposed, looking up from his ID card. There he is just as he imagined himself, among the other faces. The faces of Contreras Maluje, Don Alonso Gahona, El Quila Leo. They and all the others in the surrounding photographs grow restless when they sense his presence. They seem puzzled. They glance at the man who tortured people, eye him curiously, try to creep into his photograph to get a better look at him. In the left-hand corner, I imagine José Weibel taking off his thick glasses and rubbing his eyes, trying to see more clearly and recognize this new man who's appeared on the table. A vague memory of the day he was detained clouds his mind. Emerging from a corner under other photographs, Carol Flores approaches the man who tortured people and introduces him to the young son he's carrying in his arms, while Comrade Yuri, bare-chested, appears from the beach where he was photographed to invite him along.

Come on, Papudo, he says, let's go for a swim.

The man who tortured people doesn't know what to do.

The man who tortured people is wearing his uniform, he can't go swimming in his clothes.

The man who tortured people remembers his wife, with whom he hardly speaks; his children, with whom he no longer plays; his parents, whom he no longer sees; and he feels an uncontrollable urge to plunge into the sea. He doesn't know where he is, he can't say what beach this is, but none of that matters, and he takes off his jacket with the pair of metal eagles, then his shirt, his tie, his pants. His uniform is trodden into the sand. It looks like the sloughed-off skin of a snake, the vestige of a body that's of no use to him anymore.

We're at your beach, Papudo, he hears a shout from somewhere.

Look around and see the color of the sand, Papudo, hear the cry of the seagulls, the sound of the waves.

Suddenly everything is familiar.

At last he's part of that ancient collective celebration that he could only watch from a distance before. The man who tortured people runs naked, feels the heat of the sun on his face, feels the cool air strike his body. His toes sink into the warm black sand of the beach where he was born, and in the distance he thinks he hears one of his children laughing, playing ball. The man who tortured people reaches the edge of the sea and then he sees him. It's Quila Leo, dear Quila Leo, ducking under and splashing naked in the waves.

We're on your beach, Papudo, he says again. Your beach. Do you recognize it now?

Without a second thought, the man who tortured people dives into the sea, immersed at last in the waters of that lost planet, its only traces the tokens scattered over the table in the parish hall.

From there I hear him shouting to me.

Remember who I am, he says.

Remember where I was, remember what they did to me.

109

GHOST ZONE

I imagine him hiding on the floor of a van. I don't know what he's wearing. I don't know whether he's clean-shaven, either. It may be that he's gotten rid of that dark bushy mustache, or on the other hand, he's kept it and he has a heavy beard, too, to throw off anyone who might recognize him. Months have gone by since he gave his testimony to the reporter and the lawyer. Since then he has waited in utter seclusion until conditions were right for him to be escorted from the country. He knows that his superiors are looking for him. He knows that if he is found, he's a dead man. That's why he's being taken in secret to complete some paperwork that will make it possible for him to leave. He's hidden on the floor of a delivery van from Manantial Books, a familiar store.

There he is, under piles of packages. Schoolbooks, notebooks, boxes of pencils and erasers shifting with each turn of the wheel. He feels the weight of the bundles on his back and legs. He can hardly see out from under all the packages. From the street comes the clamor of the city. He hears car engines, horns, the radio announcer's voice. His hands are sweating. His scalp, too. The trip has taken longer than he calculated. But all at once he feels the van's motor slowing, the turn signal ticking, the clutch shifting, and all of this tells him that they're parking in front of a church. Specifically, Our Lady of Los Ángeles on Avenida El Golf, in the upper reaches of the city.

We'll wait here, he hears the lawyer say from the front of the van.

He doesn't answer, acquiescing in silence. He knows what this means, they discussed it in advance. Any moment now a car will pull up and an official will step out to take his finger-prints for his new identity. In a few days he'll be in possession of the passport that will enable him to travel south and cross the mountains into Argentina. Then he'll fly to France, where help is waiting to get him started in his new life. But it is not yet time for that. Now he simply has to keep calm and wait for the official. Everything will happen in the van. From inside the church, sympathetic eyes are watching, ready to assist. In case they're discovered, in a true emergency, the Spanish embassy a few blocks away is ready to offer them asylum. If they aren't seized on the street and they're able to reach the embassy, they'll be driven to the airport in a diplomatic car and put on a flight to Madrid. No suitcases, no goodbyes, no plan, no passport. But nobody wants a real emergency. They've taken every precaution and neither the air force nor the security services should know they're here now.

I imagine the lawyer turning on the radio as they wait. From the speakers comes a song from back then, December 1984. I try to remember what was on the radio in those days and the first thing that comes to mind is the song from the *Ghostbusters* sound track. For some reason, that's the background music I imagine for this scene. *If there's something strange / in your neighborhood / who you gonna call? Ghostbusters!* goes the chorus, over and over. And on screen I remember a young Bill

Murray with a couple of partners carrying machine guns that were actually sophisticated weapons for fighting presences that no one can see, ghostly beings that only the Ghostbusters can find and destroy with powerful rays. I doubt the lawyer would have liked this song especially, he probably never even saw the movie, but at this point taste has nothing to do with it. All that matters is seeming like someone he isn't: specifically, a driver for Manantial Books humming a pop song as he delivers packages around the city.

A car stops nearby.

In it is a clerk from the Civil Registry office.

The lawyer recognizes his contact. They exchange looks.

The clerk exits the car and climbs surreptitiously into the van. In the back, he gets to work with the man who tortured people. The process is brief, it shouldn't take them long. Pre-prepared forms, signatures, fingerprints.

The lawyer keeps a lookout. Everything seems normal out on the street. No one in the neighborhood has any idea what's happening inside the van. A woman goes by with a child in a stroller. Two grandmothers walk calmly past the church. They smile at him when their gazes meet. *If there's something strange / in your neighborhood / who you gonna call? Ghostbusters!*

A police van appears in the area.

It's moving slowly and it halts to observe the vehicle from Manantial Books.

The lawyer quickly picks up a delivery form and looks away

from the national police as they drive past. He hums the song on the radio as he pretends to work, scribbling who knows what with a pencil on an imaginary delivery list.

The cops, he warns under his breath.

In the back, the man who tortured people is sweating in the December heat and from nerves. His fingerprint won't take. The ink refuses to stick to his damp fingers and when he touches the paper, all he leaves are smears, random blurry lines. They try again. Two, three, four times, but it's no good. Despair settles over the van. For a brief moment the man who tortured people imagines that his body is dissolving. That his face is no longer his face, that he himself is only a shadow or a reflection of what he was or is. A blot as black as the ones he's leaving on one form after another. His fingerprints are essential for identification purposes, fake or not. Without them there will be no identity card to travel south to the border with Argentina, no passport to leave the country. But forms are crumpled and discarded with each failed attempt. And the more forms that are wasted, the more they sweat, the more nervous they grow, the longer the process takes, until minutes become hours. The police seem to crawl past, and it's as if they're in a parenthesis in time, as if the *Twilight Zone* stopwatch is at work and time on the street has come to a standstill.

What to do if the police decide to search the van.

What to do if they open the back doors.

What to do if they've been tipped off and they're sniffing around the neighborhood, ready to reel them in.

The lawyer thinks about the Spanish embassy. He imagines hitting the accelerator and driving at top speed until he reaches its gates, then speeding through them. He imagines himself shattering the seeming calm of this neighborhood, startling the grandmothers still walking past the church, startling the woman with the stroller. And as he imagines his abrupt exit from the country and his uncertain future in exile, his hands become sweaty, the tips of his fingers are slippery, just like the man who tortured people's, his fifth form already crumpled on the floor of the van. Five identities obliterated because of the smearing of those stubborn prints.

If there's something strange / in your neighborhood / who you gonna call?

What happens next is quick and discreet.

The clerk climbs out of the van. He's carrying the signed forms, fingerprints inked at last. His breathing is labored, his legs still trembling slightly from nerves. He gets back into the same car in which he came. In a few days they'll be in touch again, the documents ready. Without a glance at his contact, the lawyer starts the van. He accelerates gently and drives calmly down the street, without rousing suspicions. In the rearview mirror he glimpses the grandmothers and the woman with the stroller. He sees the police heading off, too. All at once, they've ceased to be a threat. From the window of their van the police are watching other people, other cars. Or maybe they aren't watching anything. They're just singing along to some song on the radio or commenting on the news of the day. They carry on with their daily rounds, never suspecting that the Manantial Books van leaving the neighborhood harbors a man with no identity, traveling hidden under piles of packages. A true ghost.

Yes, sometimes I dream of rats.
Of dark rooms and rats.
Of women and men screaming, and of letters like yours,
arriving from the future asking questions about those
screams.

I don't know what to tell you.
I don't remember anymore
what the screams say
or what the letters say.

I've just been watching a TV show called *Brain Games*. The host guides viewers through a series of exercises and situations testing their mental capacity. Meanwhile, magicians, neuroscientists, and philosophers parade across the screen, trying to explain the manifold mysteries of the human brain. The episode I just watched is about blindness and distraction. Or to put it more plainly, about how the brain sees what it wants to see. The host says that normally we assume we've seen what's in front of our eyes, but the real magic lies in what our brain does with the information. Without the meaning the brain imparts to what it arranges and interprets, what we see would be a random collection of shapes and colors. And yet this great processing capacity has its limits, the host tells us, and that's what the first game is about.

On the television we see four little soccer balls, one in each corner of the screen. The host asks us to choose a ball and focus on it. I choose the one in the upper-left-hand corner. Then I follow the instructions and I focus on it. I don't look at the other three, I just watch my little ball in the upper-left-hand corner. As I'm watching it, I hear the voice of the host describing exactly what is happening before my eyes: the other three balls begin to disappear from the screen. From one moment to the next, I see only my ball. The funny thing is that when I'm told to watch the full screen again, I realize that the other three balls were always there. My eyes saw them, but when I was focusing on a single one, my brain stopped registering the others. It turned them invisible.

During World War I, the Germans deployed one of their most fearsome weapons: the U-boat, a submarine that was difficult to target because it never came up to the surface. According to the show's host, after countless devastating attacks, the crew of a British navy ship had an unusual idea. In order to make the submarines surface so that they could be attacked, the British navy crew would disguise their vessel as a harmless cruise ship. When the submarines saw through their periscopes that there was no danger, they would rise, never imagining that an attack was imminent. To carry out this piece of trickery, the English needed a key element not present on warships: women. So it was decided that some of the crew would disguise themselves. Arm in arm with their comrades, the cross-dressing sailors strolled on deck, pretending to be half of a happy tourist couple, or two friends chatting while taking a leisurely stroll in the sea air. This wild idea succeeded. Some lens of some periscope of some submarine spotted the scene and immediately the German crew assumed there was no reason not to rise to the surface. According to the show's host, on March 15, 1917, the British bait ship attacked the first U-boat to be destroyed by this curious method.

The Germans saw men dressed as women on the deck of a warship. And yet what they processed from that image was the presence of a cruise ship. They rapidly manufactured details to fit a preconceived idea, took for granted information they didn't possess, making inferences, and misreading the facts before their eyes. Thanks to a small trick by the English, the Germans chose to see just one soccer ball.

It's the trick that makes the magic, says the host.

It doesn't matter what you see. All that matters is what you believe you see.

A few months ago, on the same screen on which I've just been watching *Brain Games*, M and I watched a special on the staged media of the dictatorship. M is the father of my son. If this were a *Brain Games* exercise, anyone who saw us going about our daily business at home would infer that he's my husband. And yet the host's voice would correct that mistake, because we aren't married. Readers who've been paying serious attention to the objective facts laid out in this book will have assumed the presence of M. Incidental or ghostly, maybe, but ultimately a real presence. He's even mentioned in one chapter as the father of the narrator's son: but has anyone spared him a single thought before we reached this point in the story? I doubt it. No one has properly imagined him. The trick has been not to focus attention on M. Until this very moment, when I instruct everyone to stop staring at the upper-left-hand corner, to watch the full screen.

M and I were lying in bed watching television. M isn't my husband but he isn't my boyfriend either. I could call him my partner, but that seems too fussy. Bereft of a word to describe our relationship, I've decided to call him M. So as I was saying, we were watching a special on staged events under the dictatorship. We're somewhat obsessed with the topic and when investigative shows like this are announced we make plans to watch them. The program undertook to cover various scenes that were staged for the purpose of shaping the truth. Lots of media outlets were used repeatedly as vehicles for disinformation and lies. In fact, Televisión Nacional de Chile, the state television station, was taken over by the military and used on this important battlefront: the manipulation of the truth, the art of making us see nothing but a single soccer ball.

The first images I remember are of an International Red Cross delegation's visit to the prison camp in Pisagua, months after the military coup. A team from Televisión Nacional filmed the visit. In the footage, we see a group of skinny, ragged prisoners swimming at the beach and playing soccer. As we watch the scene there is an interview with three detainees who say timidly that they're being treated marvelously, they feel like they're at a real vacation camp. Inevitably, M and I burst out laughing. It's a pathetic scene. Everything is crudely manipulated. It looks like a comedy skit, *Monty Python* style. A sad sketch, a cruel dark joke, but a joke nonetheless.

Then come the fake press conferences and testimonies. Alleged clashes, alleged guerrilla forces, alleged suicides, alleged discoveries of alleged stashes of weapons and documents. And among these alleged scenarios comes a staged event from 1983.

A week before, the MIR, or Revolutionary Left Movement, had mounted an attack leading to the death of the governor of metropolitan Santiago, General Carol Urzúa. The reprisals were unexpected. Agents from the CNI, the National Information Center, detained those responsible, but days later they also surrounded two MIR safe houses and killed five MIR members, presenting the occurrence to the press as a violent face-off.

M remembers this news story well. He was a boy, twelve years old, and he lived very close to Calle Fuenteovejuna, where one of the MIR safe houses was located. M says that it was early, around 8:00 p.m., when explosions were heard in the neighborhood. Truth be told, in those days explosions were not infrequent. His mother's policy was to lock the apartment door whenever there was a blackout or a helicopter flew overhead or the sound of an explosion was heard, whether near or far from the building where they lived. So the door to M's apartment was swiftly locked, as an airtight security measure, and they carried on with the evening routine. Setting the table, serving dinner, laying out clothes and school things for the next day.

M says that he expected to hear something about it on the news, but as far as he remembers, there was nothing. Later that night, a news flash interrupted the scheduled programming. This must have been when he saw the same news segment we watched in the special. A reporter states that at 1330 Calle Fuenteovejuna in the district of Las Condes, three radicals, two men and a woman, were killed after a dramatic confrontation ending in a big blaze. When the radicals realized they were trapped by the police, they decided to burn all the compromising documents they kept at the safe house, starting a fire that had yet to be extinguished at the time of reporting.

M must have seen that house when he was a boy riding

around the neighborhood on his skateboard. A single-story white brick house with a small front yard and a barred gate. But he never noticed it. His eyes saw it but his brain didn't process the information. It wasn't until that night, sitting in front of his eighties television set, that he followed instructions and concentrated on the house, on it alone, and on what the reporter's voice was saying, like everybody else watching the news.

Lying in bed, we watched the news report just as the whole country must have watched it in 1983. We observed the flurry of activity outside the house in flames. The reporter says that the radicals were intercepted by national police agents at a roadblock a few blocks from the house. The reporter says that when they were surprised they drew their guns and fled into hiding, shooting as they went. The reporter says that from inside the house, the radicals shot to kill, initiating a dramatic gun battle that fortunately hadn't injured a single man in uniform. The reporter is flanked by flares as he talks, his voice scrambled by the sound of radio transmitters, the voices of firemen, other reporters, police officers and agents walking past.

I sat up in bed, moving closer to the screen to get a better look. Everything was faded and gray, like my memories of that time. I scrutinized every inch of the picture, aware that I shouldn't overlook any corner of it, any bit of scenery. I examined every face passing before me, following each with obsessive interest, intent as a spy, because in the middle of all that activity, camouflaged in the shadows and smoke, perhaps caught for a second by the camera or hidden in the wings, I knew he was there. The man who tortured people.

Let's open that door again. Behind it we'll find another dimension. A world forever hidden by the old trick that makes us look the other way. A vast, dark territory that seems distant but is as close as the reflection we see each day in the mirror. You're crossing to the other side of the glass, is what the intense narrator of my favorite series would have said. You're entering the twilight zone.

The man who tortured people says that on September 7, 1983, they were summoned to a major operation. Around 8:00 p.m., he and a group of sixty agents arrived at the parking lot of a supermarket. As the Santiaguinos of the upper city did their shopping and loaded their cars with groceries, the sixty agents awaited instructions. The man who tortured people says that a CNI jeep drove up, mounted with a .30-caliber machine gun. A *reineta*, he calls it. A national police officer explained that the night's objective was three radicals at a safe house on Calle Fuenteovejuna. Their names were Sergio Peña, Lucía Vergara, and Arturo Villavela, also known as El Coño Aguilar, a key figure in the MIR organization. Those responsible for the death of General Carol Urzúa had already been arrested, but this action was deliberately aimed at eliminating the leadership of the movement and sending a clear message about who was in charge. The man who tortured people says that the national police officer made it clear that he didn't want a single bastard to come out of that house alive. That's what he said: no bastard is coming out of that house alive, I want everybody dead. Those were his instructions. The man who tortured people says the sixty agents left the supermarket and moved on to Calle Fuenteovejuna.

This is where M enters the story. Surely the sixty agents drove past M's building in their trucks. Surely, as my mother-in-law was making dinner up on the thirteenth floor, the sixty agents were positioning themselves a few meters from the white brick house at 1330, so close to M's building. There they set up the .30-caliber machine gun capable of firing a thousand rounds per minute and they evacuated the neighboring houses, staging the scene for the execution. Surely, as M was setting the table and laying out the forks and spoons, the sixty agents were listening over the radio for the official to give the order to start shooting.

Maybe: what were Sergio Peña, Lucía Vergara, and Arturo Villavela doing inside?

Maybe they were making dinner too. Maybe Sergio was setting the table. Maybe Arturo was cooking something for the three of them. Maybe Lucía was laying out the spoons and forks when there was a sudden hail of bullets. Maybe it was then, in that first minute of machine gun fire, that M and his family heard what they call the first explosion. Maybe they stopped what they were doing. Maybe M and his mother looked at each other in confusion and possibly even fear. Maybe it was then that my mother-in-law ran to lock the apartment door. Maybe it was then that an officer addressed 1330 Fuenteovejuna through a megaphone. Come out, he said. You're surrounded by security forces, surrender. Surely M looked out the window, trying to see what was going on, and his mother said no, move away from there, come back into the dining room, come to the table, dinner's almost ready. Maybe M obeyed, calling his siblings, just as Sergio exited the front door of 1330 Fuenteovejuna with his hands up. Surely, as M and his siblings sat down at the table, the sixty agents obeyed the order to fire again and Sergio fell to the ground, riddled with bullets. Surely it was then that some of the sixty agents threw a flare into the house and that noise plus the burst of machine gun fire sounded like a second explosion from the thirteenth floor of the apartment building where M lived. The man who tortured people says that Lucía shot back from inside and then the sixty agents opened uninterrupted fire for close to four minutes. The man who tortured people says that once the shooting stopped they entered the house and they saw Lucía and Arturo's bodies on the floor. The man who tortured people says he was ordered to drag the bodies out into the street. The man who tortured people says the bodies were exhibited like trophies before the cameras and floodlights of the press.

M comes with me to Fuenteovejuna. It's a Sunday in February and there's no one on the streets. The neighborhood is a silent, ghostly place in the oppressive 5:00 p.m. sun. A few blocks away is an empty plaza. Swings, slides, and solitary benches wait for better weather to attract someone. In the middle of the street the old trees on the median rustle at the brush of a faint breeze. The silence is filled with the soft sound of branches over our heads. There is something disturbing in the air here. I can feel it. It's as if the buildings know the story I'm telling and the landscape falls mute at the memory of it, in an attempt to make room for what our eyes can't see, for what is seemingly no longer here.

Number 1330 doesn't look much like the facade we saw burning on television. In its place is a two-story building with a tall gate and a yellow wall that reveals little of the interior. We wonder who could live in a house with such a dramatic past. Do the inhabitants know what happened there thirty-three years ago? Inside, in the middle of a small, neglected front yard, there is a truck piled high with old junk: a fan, a couple of cardboard boxes, some paint cans. I watch to see whether there's any movement within. I try to detect comings and goings, the movement of a curtain, a face looking out the window, but nothing happens. Everything is disturbingly still in the house and on the street.

I can imagine M at twelve riding his skateboard. The sound of the wheels on the pavement rattles the silent space. I imagine M at full speed on this street and that simple act brings the still scene back to life. My brain short-circuits, fills in the gray areas, tries to see past the information provided, and my mind seethes with possible ways to explore this slumbering landscape.

M on his skateboard.

Or better yet, M walking with his friends, talking and laughing.

They have a soccer ball. They're passing it as they walk. The ball shoots from place to place, shuttling into each corner of this mental image. M and his friends pass in front of 1330. They stop for a moment, about to ring the bell and run. But they don't. For some arbitrary reason, as arbitrary as any of my imaginary scenarios, they choose the house next door. M and his friends ring the bell at 1332 and dash off, fleeing with the ball, while inside 1330, Lucía, Sergio, and Arturo live a strange family life. They remain ignorant of M's pre-adolescent escapades. Ignorant of me, who is conjuring them up today, and ignorant, too, of the agents who have been watching them for three months.

I imagine Sergio on the other side of the wall. Maybe he's reading a book or smoking a cigarette or having coffee in the kitchen. Maybe he's talking to Arturo, or they're watching television, or listening to some song on the radio. Imagining, I make the walls talk. I interrogate the silent houses next door, the mute windows harboring information behind drawn curtains. Imagining, I ask the old trees to speak, I ask the cement under my feet, the lampposts, the telephone wire, the stale air circling this place. Imagining, I bring the bullet holes back to life. My mind short-circuits and in its imaginings it completes unfinished stories, reconstructs half-told tales, visualizes details that go unmentioned, ignores the instructions that I was given and watches all the corners of the screen, keeping track of every ball.

I can see Lucía sitting at the 1330 dining room table. She has pencil and paper and she's writing a birthday letter to her little girl, Alexandra, who's in France visiting her grandmother. The letter will be microfilmed and it will reach the child via some strange process that triggers no suspicions and puts no one's life in danger. In it, Lucía says she wishes she could give her daughter a hug and sing happy birthday to her in person. It's been months since she returned to Chile and she misses her little girl so much. She also writes about what's happening in their faraway country, a country no one has ever heard of. She tells her daughter about the first general strike led by copper miners. She tells her that at night people bang on pots as a symbol of their discontent and hunger. She talks about television, too, and about a show she's seen that she's sure her daughter would like a lot. It runs on the weekends. When Lucía watches it she imagines her daughter sitting next to her, eyes on the screen, laughing. It's a children's show called *The Smurfs*. It's about a city inhabited only by Smurfs, who are like little children who live in toadstool houses and play happily together in the woods. Among them is just one girl Smurf, whose name is Smurfette and who has long blond hair, the way Lucía remembers her daughter's. There is also a Papa Smurf who takes care of them, but they have no mother, she writes, foreseeing a possible future.

On the same median where M and I stand looking at the front of 1330, the man who tortured people lay Lucía's body. If we look down and use our imagination we can see her in the middle of the night, here at our feet. Her bullet-riddled body is naked, she's wearing only underpants. That's how she was photographed by the press and that's how she appeared on front pages the next day. That's how I remember her, because that's how she was shown to me, that's the instruction I was given under the headline "Radical Assassins Die in Dramatic Shoot-Out." That's how her family must have seen her, her mother over there in France, even her little girl once she wasn't little anymore. Despite the years and this whole avalanche of imagination I still can't understand why they had to undress her for that crude display. How did they pull off her dress? Who removed her bra? Who stole her watch? What about her earrings? What about the chain around her neck? What happened to those clothes? Who ended up with her things? What eyes saw those naked breasts? What hands touched the cold skin of her thighs? What words did they speak as they undressed her? What abject fantasy crossed their perverted minds? The man who tortured people never mentions any of this. In his testimony he doesn't explain or even describe the moment when Lucía was stripped of her clothes. I imagine that if he carried the body out into the street he must have taken part in the ritual. But he doesn't say so. He doesn't accept responsibility for it. He gives an instruction in his testimony, he directs me to turn my gaze elsewhere.

If this were an episode of *Brain Games*, anyone who saw M and me standing here in the street would think we're two residents of this quiet neighborhood enjoying an eccentric summer stroll under the sun's blistering rays. The viewers' eyes would see only the stillness, observing the slight rustle of the treetops and the silent facades of these houses in the upper reaches of the capital. Like those Germans on the World War I submarine, they'd view this scene through their periscope and they'd see a pleasure cruise. They wouldn't see Lucía naked on the ground waiting for a sheet to cover her at last. Based on the information in front of their eyes, they would have to accept the first explanation their brains concocted. If this were an episode of *Brain Games* the host would end the show by telling us what we already know. That a simple trick is all it takes to make us see just one ball.

Once I came back from an operation
with bloodstains on my pants.
I hadn't noticed them, but my wife did.
She asked me if I was at the massacre
that was on television,
the one with the shot-up houses
in Las Condes and Quinta Normal.

I always lied to her, but that night I couldn't.

I saw her face when I said yes.
Her face scared me.
Her silence scared me.

That night I started to dream of rats.
Of dark rooms and rats.
Rats watching me with red eyes.
Rats following me and creeping into the room with me,
slipping between
the legs of my bloodstained pants.

Mario has lunch with his father and his uncle. His father isn't his father and his uncle isn't his uncle. The names they use aren't their real names either, but in their performance of the day-to-day in this clandestine life, Mario is Mario, his father is his father, and his uncle is his uncle. Mario is in his school uniform. He's fifteen years old and he's home from school. Now that they're sitting around the table together, his uncle who isn't his uncle and his father who isn't his father ask how his day was. For Mario, this is a complicated question. A few months ago he started school again, but it hasn't been easy to get back to work, back to his books, back to homework. Also, his school isn't his school. It's a new one, different from the one before, which in turn was different from the one before that, and the one before that, and the one before that.

It was okay, he says, and neither his father nor his uncle presses him further because they know that in this role-playing game, neither fake fathers nor fake uncles should pester him.

The radio is on while they eat. The announcer reports the news of the day. Every day, Mario comes home from school and the three of them sit down for lunch and listen to the news. They probably discuss the assault on General Carol Urzúa. A week after it happened, it's still all anyone is talking about on the radio and television.

When they're finished eating, the uncle clears the table

and starts to wash the dishes. Mario and his father talk for a while longer. Maybe they talk about Mario's mother, who really is his mother, and who is the wife of his father who isn't his father. Maybe they talk about his siblings, who really are his siblings, but who in the game that is this performance have had to split up and live separate lives. They've moved to another house in another country, while he is staying in this house, which isn't his house either, though to a certain degree it is, because at the age of fifteen he's lived in so many houses that none has really been his. Or maybe they all have been, in part. The house in La Florida, the house in San Miguel, the house in La Cisterna, the house in Conchalí, the house in the parish of El Salto, where he lived with the priest. And now this house in Quinta Normal, specifically at 5707 Calle Janequeo.

Mario's mother worked for a neighborhood association in the district of La Florida. Several times, as she was on her way to a work meeting, she noticed a pair of men with mustaches and dark glasses watching her, hiding out in a taxi or a van. Worried, she gathered her four children and told them they would be moving south, to the city of Valdivia. The children accepted the decision and when the day came for the move, they said goodbye to their schoolmates, friends, and neighbors, and they got in a taxi to the bus station. On the one hand the children were sad to be leaving home, but on the other they were giddy at the prospect of going away and getting to know a faraway place. What would Valdivia be like? What would the Valdivians be like? Would it be very cold? Would it rain as much as people said?

With all these questions in mind, Mario and his siblings

rode in the taxi along unfamiliar streets toward the bus that would carry them south. From the window they saw parts of the city they had never seen before. Plazas, parks, stores, video game outlets, different people, different markets, different stands. When the car stopped at last, great was their surprise when they realized they weren't at the bus station but at a house in what they were told was the district of San Miguel. The children were silent, not understanding what was happening. They unloaded their belongings in bewilderment, and then, once they were inside, their mother explained the rules of a new game they were going to play.

This house was a special house, she said. Everything that happened from now on between these four walls would be a secret: any people who visited, any meetings that were held, any flyers that were printed, any conversations overheard. From now on, there would be things they couldn't talk about, that were part of a secret and unspoken reality, a hidden dimension that only they and nobody else could inhabit. They wouldn't go back to their neighborhood or visit their old friends, because everybody thought they were in Valdivia. The old house and the old neighborhood were part of a life that didn't exist anymore. Now they had this one, the life of the game and of secrets.

In this new life, Alejandro, alias Raúl, Mario's father-not-father, is the new piece on the game board. Alejandro and Mario's mother had met at her job and fallen in love. Now they were a family. Who would suspect a family like this, with four children who play outside, go to the school on the corner, buy ice cream at the store across the street? If one of the kids walks around with his ball, no one imagines he's inspecting the neighborhood. No one imagines that later he's giving his parents a report, letting them know whether there's a suspicious car, whether there's a stranger who might raise an alarm. If one of the kids goes out holding an adult's hand and they meet up with someone else, no one imagines that what the child is really doing is handing the adult off to a contact. No one imagines that in this house full of children, injured comrades are being cared for, comrades on the run are being sheltered, *El Rebelde* is being printed on a press set up in the back room.

But in the game of this performance, there are many returns to square one. This wasn't something their mother told them, but Mario and his siblings begin to figure it out. From the house in San Miguel, they move on to another house, then another, and another. It's as if they've landed on a square that sends them back to the start, and over and over again they find themselves in a new house, with new neighbors, embarking on a new life while keeping the old one secret.

Each new life came with a new school. And each new school required a new story to answer the questions of new friends. This story couldn't be the real one, of course, or anything like the one concocted for the previous school. Playing the game, Mario made up lives he didn't live, came up with names that weren't his, invented fake grandparents, nonexistent family members, phony birthdays, imaginary trips. Each detail of each of the versions of each of their lives had to be precisely coordinated with their siblings' and their parents' so that no one would go off script. And this had to happen at every school and every neighborhood they moved to. Each of the new squares where they landed required them to stage a performance on top of a performance. To make things up on top of what they'd already made up. The line between reality and fiction became so perilously thin, so complicated and tangled, that after a while, at each new level of the game, Mario and his siblings had to take a break from school for the sake of their own safety and mental health.

At the age of thirteen, Mario got a job in a store in the neighborhood of Patronato. He traveled there every day, conquering a new territory. Little by little the game board got bigger, and, as in Monopoly, the city was traversed and colonized by the siblings and by the game of secrets. One of Mario's brothers worked as a parking lot attendant at the National Stadium, so they were able to move their playing pieces to Ñuñoa. Then they worked as vendors in open-air markets in different districts. Then they moved to La Cisterna. Then they left La Cisterna. Then they moved to Conchalí. Then they went their separate ways and Mario ended up at a parish house in El Salto where he was taken in by a Spanish priest. Then other houses. Other neighborhoods. Other neighbors. Other friends. And so on from square to square, level to level, life to life.

As I write this, my son is celebrating his fifteenth birthday with some friends. They're in the dining room, eating and laughing. I can hear them from here. They've known each other since they were five years old. They've grown up together, gone to school together, lost their baby teeth, seen each other's pimples appear, gotten into music, sports, girls, city life, and because of all that, and other things, too, they call themselves friends now. An unbroken thread of history runs through their relationship. I'm sure there are many zones in each of them that are unknown to my son, but I have no doubt that their names are their names, their parents their parents, their houses their houses, and their lives their lives.

Mario moved into 5707 Janequeo early in 1983. The house was located across from a clinic. It was an old terraced house of adobe and brick, with two inner yards where fruit trees grew. Here they shared the game board with new players. Uncle José, whose real name was Hugo, and who wasn't really Mario's uncle; and Uncle José's wife and three children, who weren't really his cousins, though he had to treat them as if they were. Suddenly they were all living on top of each other. There were so many pieces of the game to coordinate that life in Janequeo was more fun. There were lots of kids and that summer they enjoyed the fruit trees, the plaza across the way, the pickup games in the street, the hose-offs in the yard, the big lunches at the dining room table. The old house was full of life. But despite the high spirits of the children on Janequeo, the times outside were complicated, with protests and pot-banging, and while the gang played, an unlicensed taxi parked on the corner every week to spy. Mario spotted it on his daily rounds and dutifully conveyed the information to his parents. And so, before summer was over, it was decided to attempt a strategic play. The aunt who wasn't his aunt and her three children who weren't his cousins would leave the country for Cuba, for their safety. Then, in May, a few months later, yet another new twist was introduced in the game. Mario's mother, the only real thing he had left, would leave the country. A valuable piece had to be protected and the only way to do it was to take her off the game board. His mother traveled to Cuba and his siblings followed a few months later. Mario watched them leave with their bags and suitcases, and as he did, he felt the hole they left in that big old house, which wasn't his house but a fake house, the house of a fake family with a fake life. There would be no more big lunches cooked for everyone by Uncle José, no more afternoons in front of the TV, or pickup games in the street, or hose-offs in the back yard. The game board was beginning to empty. For some reason, Mario didn't leave. He stayed behind at 5707 Janequeo with Hugo, alias Uncle José, and Alejandro, alias his father Raúl, far from his real mother and his real siblings, carrying on the role-playing game, continuing the performance every day, until this very moment, at the table after dinner on September 7, 1983.

At 16:30 the first important move of the afternoon is made: Alejandro, alias Raúl, Mario's father-not-father, kisses him goodbye on the forehead and leaves the house. He'll be back later, he says.

At 16:35, Hugo, alias Uncle José, sits down with Mario in the living room and talks to him about his life as a student in Argentina, where he's from. It's a nice moment, but at 17:00, Mario goes to his room to try to study, because in this life of performances, trying to be a good student helps a lot.

At 18:00, Mario closes his books and thinks that Alejandro,

alias Raúl, his father who isn't his father, has been gone for an awfully long time.

At 19:50, Mario is hungry and leaves his room.

At 19:55, Mario runs into Hugo, alias Uncle José, in the kitchen, making banana shakes.

At 20:00, Hugo, alias Uncle José, says he's worried that Alejandro, alias Raúl, has been out too long, as he pours two banana shakes.

At 20:05, Mario and Hugo, alias Uncle José, sit down to watch the TV news.

At 20:10, Mario gets up because the news is boring and goes to his room to listen to music.

At 20:15, Mario puts a Los Jaivas tape on his cassette player and starts to listen to Gato Alquinta singing one of his songs.

At 20:30, Mario hears shots in the neighborhood. He doesn't turn down the volume or turn off the music. Gunshots, helicopters, and bomb blasts are something he's heard occasionally in every neighborhood where he's lived in previous lives, so there's no reason to worry this time.

At 20:35, Mario hears shouts.

At 20:36, Mario hears a burst of machine gun fire and he realizes that they're shooting at the house. Instinctively he drops to the floor.

At 20:37 he begins to see smoke filtering under the door to his room. At 20:40 he goes out into the dark hallway to look for Hugo, alias Uncle José. Uncle, he shouts toward the bedroom, but no one answers. At 20:41 he hears voices. At 20:42 he realizes they're the voices of agents. At 20:43 he hears another burst of gunfire. At 20:44 he can't figure out how he's still alive after the shooting and he runs down the dark, smoke-filled hallway looking for Hugo, alias Uncle José. At 20:45 he realizes his uncle isn't in his bedroom or the kitchen. He can't find him anywhere. Uncle, he shouts, uncle, but again there's no response. At 20:46 he thinks about curling up on the floor and not moving, no matter what, but at 20:47 he decides no, he can't abandon himself to his fate, he has to escape, no matter where, get out of there before he's killed by another round of machine gun fire. At 20:48 he's in the back yard. At 20:49 he's scaling the side wall; at 20:50, as he's climbing, he thinks about Alejandro, alias Raúl, his father who isn't his father, thinking how lucky it was that he didn't come back. The delay saved him, he thinks, and at 20:51 he lands in the yard of the house next door, still hearing shots and the voices of agents, who are kicking down doors and overturning furniture at 5707, while he, at 20:52, tries to scramble over the next wall to keep fleeing from yard to yard. But at 20:53 he realizes that this new wall is too high, he's tired, his body is shaking, it isn't so easy to escape the house, life weighs heavily on him, he's not going to make it. At 20:54 he decides to knock on the window of the neighbor, who at 20:55 comes out into the back yard when he hears knocking and sees the figure of a boy of fifteen asking for help, scared.

That's my house, says the boy, at 20:56.

Where it's happening, that's my house, he says, at 20:57, and he repeats the same thing at 20:58 and 20:59. My house, my house, my house, and each repetition is uttered with the conviction of someone telling the truth.

Inevitably the fifteen-year-olds get mixed up in my head. I think about Mario on that September night in 1983. Maybe he'd have a good time with my son and his friends here. In a life he never had, we would sit him down at the table to eat a piece of cake and tell him he could stay as long as he wanted. Tell him he didn't have to keep climbing wall after wall.

Andrés Antonio Valenzuela Morales, alias the man who tortured people, says he was there. After he hauled the body of Lucía Vergara out to the Calle Fuenteovejuna median, he received orders to head with his team to the other side of the city, to the district of Quinta Normal, specifically 5707 Calle Janequeo. He says it before my eyes, on the computer screen, in a video recording made in France, probably at the end of the eighties.

He's sitting in a dark café. He has long hair, nothing like in the photos I've seen of him. Thick, abundant hair. He seems like another person. Next to him is Ricardo Parez, MIRista in exile, comrade of Alejandro Salgado, alias Raúl, and Hugo Ratier, alias José. Ricardo watches him as he drinks from a glass of wine or water. The man who tortured people is smiling and answering Parez's questions, because this is an interview. Somewhat informal, with a do-it-yourself feel, but it will serve as evidence for a possible lawsuit concerning Fuenteovejuna and Janequeo, in the distant country that Chile has become in this new life they've both adopted. That's why Parez asks him to repeat some things more clearly. That he was ordered to kill everyone living in both houses, for example. That the intent was always to eliminate them, at the Fuenteovejuna house and the Janequeo house both. That it was well known they weren't directly responsible for the death of General Carol Urzúa. That these killings were a kind of vendetta.

The man who tortured people repeats what he's said more clearly, as requested, accustomed to following orders. Both men seem somewhat uncomfortable, but they try to break the ice, speaking in a casual way that sounds strained. Parez asks the man who tortured people about his nickname, Papudo, and the man who tortured people explains that in military service all his friends were from the south and he was the only one from the central coast, which is why they called him Papudo. And the two of them laugh and it's strange when they laugh. I think they feel a little stupid themselves, or that's how it seems.

French tango music can be heard beneath their words. The man who tortured people says that by the time he and his team got to Janequeo the operation had already begun. Everybody was shooting, he says. The same jeep mounted with a machine gun on Fuenteovejuna was in the middle of the street doing its job against the facade of 5707, which was where the MIRistas Hugo Ratier, alias José, and Alejandro Salgado, alias Raúl, supposedly lived.

The man who tortured people says that a few minutes after he got there he saw a person walking down the street with bags of groceries. The person stopped to see what was going on. It was a man. He could have been any local resident, but he was rapidly identified as Alejandro Salgado. When Alejandro, alias Raúl, the father-not-father of Mario, saw a group of agents shooting at the house that wasn't his house, he started to run, fleeing in terror, at the same moment Mario was climbing the wall in the back yard. Alejandro passed the truck where the man who tortured people was stationed. The man who tortured people says he watched him go by, crouching down as the rest of the officers opened fire.

He fell near a plaza.
He wasn't armed, but an officer went up and put a gun in his hand.
That's how he appeared in the newspapers the next day.
Lying on the ground with the gun, as if he'd been shooting.
I saw it.

There was a special report that night about a violent clash. Mario might have seen it on the neighbor's TV. As he heard voices and movement on the other side of the wall, he would've seen images of his house on the screen. There were police and armed agents walking the halls. On the dining room table where he'd eaten lunch a few hours ago, with the orange-flowered tablecloth, there were papers, lots of fake IDs, and a serious pile of weapons he'd never seen before. Grenades, ammunition, machine guns, pistols. If there had been a gun in the house, we would have used it to defend ourselves, thought Mario. Reporting live with a microphone in his hand, the announcer gestured at the weapons and documents, announcing that security forces had killed two dangerous terrorists in a deadly face-off.

The man who tortured people says that when they got to the house the neighbors told them there was a boy. The man who tortured people says they found Hugo Ratier's body on the floor, but the boy wasn't there.

Mario spent the night hidden at the neighbor's house, a few meters from the scene of the crime. Early the next morning, he and the neighbor left by the back door and walked to the bus stop. The facade of 5707 was full of bullet holes, the windows smashed, window frames splintered, the door ajar. Mario eyed it all furtively, as if he were just another neighbor, as if it hadn't been his house, as if he hadn't lived his last life there. National police officers were still on the street, but no one noticed him. No one was looking for him or asking what had happened to the kid. It was as if he had never existed. As if having vanished into the game and the secret for so long he had become a secret himself.

They took a bus to the neighborhood of Mapocho, and got some breakfast. When they were done, the neighbor brought Mario to the repair shop where he worked. He told Mario that if he needed anything he'd be here. Then he gave him a little money and they parted.

Mario walked aimlessly around the center of Santiago. Without realizing it, he came to the Plaza de Armas, ground zero of the game board. Centerpoint of any game. Here everything was functioning normally, as if nothing had happened. People were going about their business, buses filled the streets, the stores were beginning to open, old people were feeding the pigeons. For a brief moment he wished he was one of these people. Having a life instead of an endless list, so hard to manage and remember. Going to a single school, then maybe getting some kind of degree, finding a job, settling down with a woman who would call him by his name, moving into a house and not budging for at least a decade. Having children he wouldn't have to wake up in the night to go on the run, children who would celebrate their fifteenth birthdays with friends, with birthday cake.

At a newsstand he saw the daily papers and read the headlines. On one front page there was a photograph of Alejandro. He was lying on his back, his face bloody, a gun next to his right hand. It was him: his father-not-his-father. The same person who until yesterday had lived with him in the house that wasn't his house, living a life of lies, though in light of what had happened, it was the only life he had. Mario was tempted to use the little money the neighbor had given him to buy a couple of newspapers. To keep these photographs as memory or proof, but he quickly changed his mind. His only guidelines were the game and the secret, and now that there were no clear rules to follow, no squares to move back to, he was at the start again.

In his head, Mario rolled the dice and lost himself in the city.

Yes, sometimes I dream of rats.
Of dark rooms and rats.
Of men and women screaming
and of letters from the future
asking about the screams.

I don't remember anymore
what the screams say
or what the letters say
All that's left are the rats.

I went to a psychiatrist
to get rid of them.
She sent me for an encephalogram.
I saw an X-ray of my head.
I looked for the rats so I could cut them out with scissors,
but they weren't there, they were hiding in the shadows.

They made me stack cubes,
they made me take tests.
They said the rats were there
because I was worried about money.
They said I was tense, nervous,
that a few pills would help.

I never told them what was happening to me.
I never told them about my job and how it was sickening me.
They were doctors from the intelligence service,
I couldn't tell them the truth.

Then I couldn't take it anymore.
I went to the magazine and I did what I did.

You've told it better than I could.
Your imagination is clearer than my memory.

As a girl I had a weakness for ghost stories. I lived in a big old house that creaked at night, and in my childhood fantasies, it was overrun by spirits. I saw shadows cross the hallway at midnight and I heard the tap of feet on the parquet floor. I heard nonexistent people laughing and talking in the back bedroom. I heard furniture being moved, vases breaking, brooms sweeping. Whether it was all real or a childish delusion I'll never know, but because of my imaginings as a girl, I guess, I developed a perverse connection to stories about lost souls. I had such a kindred feeling for the stories, it was as if they had been written for me. As soon as I learned to read I immersed myself in books about ghosts. The books came to me by chance, at random: from the bookcase at home, the shelves of some friend, or a reading list handed out by the teacher at school. I remember the elderly phantom in *The Canterville Ghost*. Murderer of his wife, lord and master of the house he has inhabited for centuries, he battles the modern ways of the Otis family, who scoff at him, show no fear, and use detergent to wipe away the terrible bloodstains from the killing of Lady Eleanor. And I remember Ichabod Crane, riding at night in the town of Sleepy Hollow, fleeing the headless horseman who seeks to kill him. And the ghost of Catherine in *Wuthering Heights*, calling through the fog to her beloved Heathcliff. And the young brother and sister haunted by spirits in *The Turn of the Screw*. And Ana María, in *The Shrouded Woman*, reflecting back on her life from the coffin at her own wake. I remember dreaming of the sinister House of Usher and its furniture bolted to the floor, and the "nevermore" of the raven that appeared at midnight, evoking the ghost of beloved Lenore.

That's how I imagine the man who tortured people: as one of the characters in those books I read as a girl. A man beset by ghosts, by the smell of death. Fleeing from the horseman trying to behead him or from the raven perched on his shoulder, whispering daily in his ear: nevermore.

Now he's on a southbound bus to Bariloche. He's surrounded by Mapuche peasants, fellow travelers. In the pocket of his jacket he has his new ID and passport, ready to be used for the first time when he crosses the Andes into Argentina. Behind him or in front of him, not especially close by, is another lawyer from the Vicariate. The man who tortured people has never met him, but he knows who he is because they're the only two passengers on the bus who aren't Mapuche. They've exchanged glances from their seats, but they haven't spoken to each other. The lawyer is traveling to protect him. If any problem arises during the border crossing, if the international police stop him, if the fake passport is spotted, if somehow the air force or the security services discover his whereabouts and the operation to get him out of the country, the lawyer will have to step in and do what he can to keep things on track. But there isn't much he can do, and both of them know it. If the intelligence agents get wind of his departure, they'll almost certainly be in serious trouble.

The man who tortured people tries not to think about that. He's been inside in hiding for months. Now he lets his mind wander over the bright landscape he sees through the window. The fields and cows have been left behind, as has Lake Puyehue, and now, I imagine, they're making their way into the mountains. The sky is cloudy. Small white feathers float gently in the air, that's what he sees. The feathers spin a few times before landing in the treetops, the bushes, the grass, the pastures. It's snow. The man who tortured people has probably never seen it before, but the truth is I don't know that. I simply imagine that as he watches the flakes falling more and more thickly, blotting out the landscape, he might feel the childish surprise of someone seeing snow or the sea for the first time.

"Jingle Bells" plays over the bus's speakers. It's December, and in just a few days it will be Christmas. That's probably why all the Mapuche peasants around him are traveling, because the holidays are coming and they're on their way to visit family. They've brought the usual gifts, the chickens for Christmas Eve dinner, the bottles of aguardiente and red wine. Everyone on the bus knows the song and their lips move slightly as they sing to themselves, bobbing their heads in time to the music, while outside it snows, and, in his seat, the man who tortured people thinks about the strange Christmas that awaits him if he succeeds in fleeing the country.

One of the ghost stories I remember most fondly is Dickens's *Christmas Carol*. Everybody knows the plot. Bitter old Ebenezer Scrooge is visited for Christmas by three spirits: Christmas Past, Christmas Present, and Christmas Yet to Come. With them he sets off on a strange journey, half dream and half memory, in which he witnesses different Christmas scenes that have been a part of his life. Or are, or will be.

I imagine the man who tortured people sitting on the bus, remembering the ghosts of his own Christmases. A tree strung with lights that blink on and off at his childhood home in Papudo. Twinkling lights that still shine bright in memory. His parents, his siblings, maybe an uncle or aunt and some cousins, all sitting around the table, talking, laughing, eating special dishes of chicken or beef prepared by his mother. Country people like the Mapuche on the bus with him. Happy to share a night in the tinkling glow of those Christmas lights, blinking in time to "Jingle Bells."

Another memory assails him. Like a blaze of light from that old Christmas tree, picture and sound come to him. It's the voice of the nation's first lady, Doña Lucía Hiriart de Pinochet, addressing the whole country on a state radio station. He listens to her over the radio transmitter at Remo Cero, or maybe Nido 20, or the AGA, from the chill of any jail, any secret prison. It's Christmas Eve and he's on guard duty. Prisoners and guards alike are immersed in silence, no carols or "Jingle Bells." This woman's voice fills the space with good wishes for all Chileans. She talks about the importance of family, of loved ones, of this special and symbolic day. She talks about the baby Jesus, the manger, the cows, the pigs, the donkey, Mary, the Three Kings, the little star of Bethlehem, Christmas magic, and the all-powerful love of God.

On this Christmas, or maybe a different one, a guard was

inspired to do a good deed. Probably he had been visited by some ghost of his own Christmases, and, in a humanitarian gesture, he went around opening the cell doors and bringing out the longest-serving prisoners to dine with the guards that night. I don't know what kind of food was served for Christmas dinner in a detention center. Probably the same thing as always, but being free for a moment and sharing a plate of whatever it was must have made the dinner different, I imagine. Maybe there was a bottle of wine. Maybe some milky, aguardiente-spiked *cola de mono* and Christmas cake. Maybe someone lit a candle. Maybe everyone sat back and talked, sticking to subjects that erased differences. They probably recalled past Christmases, gifts given and received. Guards and prisoners developed close relationships, having spent so long together. They were bound by a strange kind of intimacy, which, I imagine, let them enjoy a special moment that night. But the gathering didn't last long. The unit head showed up in the middle of the night and caught them in their forbidden Christmas celebration. The candle was abruptly blown out. The bottle of wine was corked and Christmas cake and *cola de mono* were cleared from the table. The party ended all at once and the prisoners went back to their cells, while the guard responsible lost his job and was expelled from the air force.

The third specter to appear to Ebenezer Scrooge is the Ghost of Christmas Yet to Come. This spirit is draped in a black robe that covers its head, its face, and the rest of its body. Only its outstretched hand is visible, the index finger pointing forward. If it hadn't been for this hand, the specter would have been hard to see in the dark of night. Though accustomed to the presence of ghosts, Scrooge was so afraid of this mysterious spirit that he could barely stand.

Ghost of the future, he said, I fear you more than any specter I have seen. But as I hope to live to be another man than what I was before, I'm prepared to see what you have to show me.

What follows is a walk around the city at night. Scrooge and the ghost hear a kind of vast murmur, the conversations of people in the street. All are talking about the recent death of someone who doesn't seem to have been well liked. No one weeps for him or mourns his departure. Christmas, they think, will be better this year now that he's vanished from the face of the earth. Before Scrooge can find out whose death they are talking about, the ghost brings him before the lonely body. The man is wrapped in a shroud, his face hidden. The room where he lies is dismal and sad. There are no flowers, no candles. No one is sitting with the dead man, no one is keeping him company, only the rats that begin to creep into the room. It's a disturbing, painful picture. Scrooge tries to understand the meaning of what the ghost is showing him, but before he can, he's whisked somewhere else.

Suddenly he finds himself in a humble abode. It is the home of Bob Cratchit, clerk at Scrooge's counting house. A man he has never bothered to learn anything about, despite the many years they've worked together. Scrooge sees Bob in a child's room. He is sitting on a chair weeping to himself as he looks around. A small crutch on the bed tells Scrooge that the clerk's ailing son has been dead for some time. In this scene from Christmas yet to come, Bob has come to the room to weep alone, so that the rest of the family doesn't have to be sad.

Then Bob sits down at the table with his children and his wife. He makes everyone promise they will never forget Tiny Tim, which is what the boy was called. No matter how many years go by, we won't forget this parting, he says. We'll always remember how patient and good he was, and we won't quarrel among ourselves over foolish things, because valuing our time together is the Christmas gift that your brother left us.

In his invisible state, Scrooge watches. The scene is sad, but it's as luminous as the candles on the Cratchits' table. The boy isn't here, but his presence is felt. Something seems to click in Ebenezer Scrooge's mind, or maybe his icy heart, as he recalls that lonely body, its sadness untouched by the glow of this house.

Specter, something tells me that we will soon part ways, says Scrooge. But first I must know the name of that poor man we saw lying dead.

The Ghost of Christmas yet to come points its finger and conveys Ebenezer Scrooge to a different time with no clear connection to the scenes that came before, a future moment edited at his own random production table. This time, Scrooge ends up at a cemetery. To his surprise he finds himself at an iron gate, accompanied by the specter, who keeps pointing forward. The horrible person hated by all, the person whose name he is about to learn, is buried here. The spirit stands among the graves and points to one of them. Scrooge advances, trembling, but before he moves closer he asks the immutable spirit, who never replies, whether what he's seen tonight is the shadow of things to come or only the shadow of things that might be.

The paths that men take in life foretell their ends, says Scrooge. But if a man turns onto a different path, will his end change?

The specter doesn't answer. It is silent, pointing to the grave. Scrooge walks toward it, and, following the specter's finger to a neglected and dirty gravestone, he reads his own name: Ebenezer Scrooge.

When I read this book, my teacher gave us an assignment. We had to write an essay telling the story of two Christmases. One that we remembered and one that we imagined in some likely future. I don't remember what I wrote. Probably something about one of those seventies Christmases shredding wrapping paper under the bright, lavishly decorated tree at my cousins' house. Or maybe a fantasy about some Christmas to come in the eighties. Maybe I imagined some present I hoped to get or some special holiday food. I'd be lying if I said I thought about what Christmas Eve was like in the secret prisons, the detention centers. I'd be lying if I said I imagined what Christmas was like for people who had lost someone to one of those cells, some gun battle, a torture session, an execution, or whatever it was. Did those families get together to celebrate? Did they open presents? Did they have a plastic tree like mine? A plastic nativity scene like mine? A plastic baby Jesus like mine?

I'd like to imagine that on that December afternoon in 1984 as he's fleeing the country and nervously making his way to

Argentina among all those country folk excited about the holidays, with their gifts in suitcases and baskets, their dreams of Christmas trees and strings of lights made in China, their humming of "Jingle Bells" in a snowy landscape like the ones in glass globes with sleds and Santas, the man who tortured people is visited by the terrible Ghost of Christmas Present. Sitting in his seat with his gaze lost in the snow, he spares a moment, a brief moment, for thoughts of the Flores family, the Weibels, the Contreras Malujes, the children of El Quila Leo, the children of Comrade Yuri, the children of El Pelao Bratti, the children of Lucía Vergara, Sergio Peña, Arturo Villavela, Hugo Ratier, and Alejandro Salgado. Tables set for dinner, with someone present to remember the missing. Empty rooms where a father can sit alone and weep so that the rest of the family doesn't have to be sad.

The bus reaches the border and everyone has to get out at the customs checkpoint. Suitcases and baskets are searched and all passengers are required to show their identification papers to the customs officers. I don't know how long the process takes, but I do know that each name is called out by an officer going down the list and asking to see IDs. Loncomilla, Catrilef, Epullanca, Newuan, Kanukeo, Antivilo. Mapuche names, Mapuche faces. The officer checks the information, consults his list, glances at each face and matches it to the ID in his hand. And he goes on, calling those who are left. Loncomilla, Catrilef, Epullanca, Newuan, Kanukeo, Antivilo. And then he speaks the name of the lawyer who's traveling as a safeguard. It echoes in the room.

The lawyer and the man who tortured people exchange brief, imperceptible looks. The lawyer steps forward with his ID and takes his turn. He smiles at the officer, waits for the latter to consult, check, confirm and then retrieves his ID. Next come more names, more IDs, more faces, until at last the officer calls the fake name of the man who tortured people.

He and the lawyer don't even try to exchange glances.
They feign indifference.

The man who tortured people steps forward. With careful, practiced nonchalance he hands over his ID. No one in the room can be allowed to suspect how nervous he is. Despite the cold his hands are sweating. His heart is beating fast, like the drum in the Christmas carol. The officer glances at the ID, as he has done with other passengers. He scans, checks his list, confirms that the photograph matches the person standing in front of him.

The lawyer watches from a distance. It's harder for him to pretend; he has less training. His right leg is quivering imperceptibly. Maybe his right eyelid, too. He feels his stomach clench. Hands, neck, back: every part of him is sweating. He knows that this is the moment. If anything goes wrong, he'll have to act, have to shout: I'm a lawyer from the Vicariate, wherever they're taking Agent Valenzuela, I'm going with him, I won't let anything happen to him.

But the gesture is unnecessary. From his corner he watches the officer return the ID to the man who tortured people. Thank you, the officer seems to say, and the man who tortured people takes his ID and puts it in his wallet. This time he does exchange looks with the lawyer from across the room. It's a brief but distinct acknowledgment, meaning they've passed the test, everything seems to be going as planned.

The officer folds the list and goes into an office. The passengers wait for their baggage to finish being checked so they can get back on the bus. It's cold. The man who tortured people lights a cigarette. From the distance, the lawyer follows suit. Maybe there's a place to buy coffee. Maybe they've already bought some. Maybe they sip from plastic cups as each imagines what's to come. A flight to Buenos Aires, a meeting with Argentinean contacts, then another flight to France touching down in a new life, a place where he can finally shake off the smell of death and get rid of that stupid raven following him everywhere with its *nevermore*.

From the customs agents' office, the fake name of the man who tortured people is heard. The officer has come to the door and is calling him again. It's his name, he hears it clearly a second time. This isn't a nightmarish fantasy, or an arbitrary invention of mine to make the scene more suspenseful. It's the honest truth. For some reason the policeman is calling just him. Him alone, no other passenger.

The man who tortured people and the lawyer look at each other.

Both turn pale when they hear the call.

No longer nonchalant or feigning indifference, the man who tortured people puts out his cigarette and approaches the officer. The vision of a gravestone with his name on it appears to him as he pulls his fake ID from his jacket pocket again. *Andrés Antonio Valenzuela Morales*, chiseled on a bleak and lonely gravestone that he can see clearly in some cemetery of the future. Or maybe it isn't a gravestone and it's just his naked, bullet-riddled corpse borne along by the river's current.

Not nonchalant in the slightest, and utterly unable to feign indifference, the lawyer watches the man who tortured people and the officer. The two of them exchange words he can't hear. He senses the moment has come to step in. He feels an urge to vomit; maybe his vision clouds. He doesn't see a gravestone or his bullet-riddled body. The future is simply blank. In the grip of this emptiness, he walks toward the man who tortured people, who is still talking to the officer. The rapid beat of his heart governs his steps, his breathing, his thoughts. I'm a lawyer of the Vicariate, he'll say. I won't let anything happen to Agent Valenzuela. But he has yet to speak when the man who tortured people pockets his ID and gestures decisively for him to retreat.

The lawyer changes direction. He doesn't slacken his pace or momentum, he just turns, as if he intended to head somewhere else. Meanwhile, the man who tortured people is saying goodbye to the agent, who goes back into his office.

Two cigarettes lit urgently at the same time.

One raised to the lips of the man who tortured people, the other to the lawyer's lips.

Tension begins to release its grip on their muscles as they inhale and exhale tobacco smoke. The man who tortured people has no way of explaining what happened, but from a distance he tries to transmit signs of reassurance. His ticket was booked twice, so his fake name was on the customs officers' list twice. A small misunderstanding they wanted to clear up, that's all.

The driver announces that they can get back on the bus. The suitcases are already loaded on top and all the passengers begin to climb aboard. The man who tortured people and the lawyer get in separately, avoiding making eye contact with each other, making no signs that might be detected. When everyone is in their seats, the bus pulls away and sets off on its route, this time through Argentine territory. Chile is left behind. An unsettling sense of freedom begins to rise through every pore of his skin, but he won't give himself permission to feel it. He knows there's still a long way to go. Hours of travel by bus and then by plane. Years of life. He'd rather distract himself by looking out the window. The landscape unfurls before them, even more luminous. Light bounces off the snow and everything goes white like in those absurd movies where people go to heaven when they die, with hopes of a new life.

Will there be a new life for him?

Will he be able to change the shadows of things to come?

He wants to believe he will, that he has the right to a change of skin. But as he's thinking, he looks out the window and sees that same old raven again, flying over the bus and shrieking louder than ever. Nevermore, he hears from his seat. Nevermore.

I'm living a new life.
Hiding from the world in my very own rat trap.
I don't use email, I don't give out my address,
no one knows how to find me.
How you were able to write me, I don't know.
How you were able to get a letter to me, I don't know.

Why do you want to write a book about me?
I've answered so many questions in the past.
Will I have to keep answering questions in the future?

I don't have much time.
I know sooner or later they'll come.
No matter where I hide.
No matter how long it's been.
It'll be quick, maybe even before I know it.
They'll have the red eyes of a devil dreaming.
They'll find me here or wherever I am,
and one of them will be willing
to stain their pants with my blood.

Maybe it'll be you.
Maybe you've done it already, there in the future.
Nothing is real enough for a ghost.

What else can I tell you?
I gather mushrooms in the woods, I read in the evenings.
And at night I dream of rats.

ESCAPE ZONE

I remember her at the back of the classroom, sitting at one of those wooden desks in the last row. The science teacher is taking attendance, ready to tell us about Major Yuri Gagarin. Or maybe it isn't him, maybe it's the Spanish teacher, who has us reading Charles Dickens. Or the math teacher, or the art teacher, or any of the other teachers, reading our last names from the class roster as we listen and call out in reply. Elgueta, here. Fernández, here. And she always comes after me on the list. González, here. Her roster number was fifteen and her full name could be read embroidered in red thread on the bib of her checkered smock: Estrella González Jepsen.

Those were days of numbers and last names. That's essentially what we were, a last name and a number on a long list of children. That long list was added to another long list, which in turn was added to yet another long list, and all those lists together were the classes that lined up early every Monday morning in the courtyard to start the week with a civic ceremony. Somebody stood up front and gave a short speech based on what the week held in store: National Police Day, Naval Victories Day, Battle of Maipú Day, Disaster of Rancagua Day, or any other heroic deed that fit the bill, and then the national anthem played over the speakers as the flag was raised. Everybody sang the anthem, the verse with the line "Your names, brave soldiers, who have been Chile's mainstay / they are engraved on our breasts" (laughter among the rows of the littlest kids) "and our children will know them too."

I suppose that's who we were: our children.

My school was a strange one, part public and part private. It started as a private school for young ladies in 1914, where the then-distinguished residents of Barrio Matta, in the heart of Santiago, sent their daughters to study with the nuns. The school had a big yard with a statue of the Virgen del Carmen in a grotto. Behind the Virgen, a long fence ran across the whole yard. On the other side of the fence was a public school attended by the not-so-distinguished residents of the neighborhood. These less well-to-do neighbors around the intersection of Nataniel Cox and Victoria sent growing numbers of children to the public school, and, across the fence, the stuck-up young ladies prayed to the Virgen, who was completely unaware that there were other children behind her back.

It was a time of fences, and virgins too.

But in the eighties everything changed. The Ministry of Education came up with the idea of decentralizing oversight of private and public schools, leaving it to the municipalities. On top of issuing business licenses and traffic permits, on top of worrying about garbage trucks, maintenance and decoration of public plazas, repair of potholes, regulation of street markets and a thousand other things, municipalities were charged with a new responsibility: education. A state subsidy was allocated, to be administered by the municipalities. No distinction was made between private and public education, thus creating two types of subsidized institutions: municipal schools, run by the district where each was located, and subsidized private schools, run by private entities. Each school was allotted a certain amount of money per student to aid in their education. So my school took down the fence in the courtyard, the students were mixed, and the school became a subsidized private institution. There was no divide anymore. We were all equal in the eyes of the state, and each of us would bring in a small sum to cover the cost of our education. It had been a while since the neighborhood stopped being distinguished, and there were no wealthy neighbors anymore who could pay the registration fee and tuition, so it made sense to accept this new form of assistance. As a result, classes grew to almost forty-five students and we ourselves didn't know everyone in the room. A sea of children, all in uniform, we clung to our numbers and our last names in order not to be shipwrecked.

I don't know whether González arrived before or after this metamorphosis. Hard to remember all the faces, all the names. There's a photograph I've kept, proof of her presence back then. In it, we must be about ten, and we're standing side by side, with the whole class. González is dressed as a ship's mate, same as me. We're wearing little white sailor hats that say Chilean Navy and we have mustaches that were painted on with burnt cork. We look alike, all forty-five of us, in blue uniforms with sailor hats and charcoal mustaches. We're on a stage decorated with colored paper to look like a big ship, and in the middle of our group, Muñoz, black cork beard and sword in hand, gives a heroic speech. "Gentlemen, we are outmatched," says our captain and we gaze at him with patriotic eyes. "But be brave and take heart. Our flag has never fallen in the face of the enemy and I hope that this day will be no different. While I live, the flag will fly, and if I die, my officers know their duty. Long live Chile, damn it," and Muñoz sets out to board the enemy ship. Every year, on the twenty-first of May, we put on this performance. Like déjà vu, it's up to us to die yet again on the enemy deck for our nation and our honor. Like last year, and the year before, and the year before that.

Let me interrupt my own reverie.

I should make a connection here to the man who tortured people. Follow the rule that I set for myself and uncover the strange, twisted link between him and González, a link close or far in a long, heavy chain like the kind dragged by Dickens's ghosts or prisoners at a secret jail. But I won't. I'll focus on other parts of the screen. I'll extend the borders of the twilight zone and I'll go right on with this story of little soldiers and big charcoal mustaches of burnt cork.

González was quiet. She didn't talk much, or if she did I don't remember. She sat at the back of the classroom, half-hidden, writing letters on graph paper from her math notebook, passing them later to my friend Maldonado. They wrote to each other and told each other secret, important things in those letters. Like about González's father's accident. Her father was an officer and a gentleman in the service of our nation. No one knew him very well; he never came to school festivals, weekly Mass, or parent meetings, but a few people had gotten a glimpse of him and they said he was a big man with gray hair, quiet like González. The accident was at work. Another officer happened to pick up a grenade, and somehow the pin got pulled. To save the officer's life, González's father grabbed the grenade with his left hand, poor little hand, and tried to throw it far away, and before he could, the grenade went off. After that, instead of a poor little left hand, González's father had a wooden hand in a black glove.

It was a time of grenades and poor little left hands, too.

The years went slowly by. Time dragged, with endless evenings of TV watching, of *Cine en su casa*, *Sábado gigante*, *Lost in Space*, *The Twilight Zone*, and of Atari, gangs of us playing *Space Invaders*. The green glow-in-the-dark bullets of the earthlings' cannons scudded up the screen until they hit an alien. The little Martians descended in blocks, in perfect formation, shooting their projectiles, waving their octopus or squid tentacles, but they always ended up exploding, like González's father's left hand. Ten points for each Martian in the first row, twenty for the ones in the second row, and forty for the ones in the back row. And when the last one died, when the screen was blank, another alien army appeared from the sky, ready to keep fighting. They gave up one life to combat, then another, and another, in a cycle of endless slaughter. Projectiles flew back and forth, as if in the kind of heroic act that we celebrated at our school assemblies and flag-raisings.

It was a time of projectiles and slaughter, too.

At some point we stopped going to the Monday assemblies. We stayed in the classroom, listening from the distance to what was happening in the yard. When the monitor made us attend, we lined up with everybody else but we didn't sing along to the verse beginning "Your names, brave soldiers." Instead we shouted the line "Be either the tomb of the free or a refuge from oppression." That was how we grew up, yelling the word *free* and the word *oppression* at the top of our lungs every Monday morning, as we organized the first meetings of our student union and got up the courage to walk out the front door of the school, heading into the street in a pack as if charging aboard an enemy ship.

It was a time of marches and protests. It was a time of *Cauce* magazine getting passed from one person to another. It was a time of shocking headlines. A time of attacks, kidnappings, strikes, crimes, scams, lawsuits, indictments. A time of ghosts, too. Of mustached monsters giving testimony in powder blue pull-out sections under the title I TORTURED PEOPLE. A time of TV specials on torture. A time of dark rooms, of women locked up with rats. Whole nights spent dreaming of those dark rooms and those rats. A time of spray-painted graffiti on walls, and leaflets we cranked out on a mimeograph machine and distributed in the streets. A time of banners, assemblies, petitions, meetings of the Secondary Students Federation at a warehouse on Calle Serrano. A time of our first militant actions, first sit-ins, first detentions. A time of lists. Long lists that we searched for the whereabouts of friends who'd been arrested. A time of heavy down parkas to protect us from the rifle butts and boots of the national police. A time of lemons, salt, the smell of tear gas, jets of water mixed with gas that not only soaked you and knocked you down, but also left you with a stink of rot that lingered for days. A time of leaders. I remember one of them standing on a fountain in the middle of the Alameda declaiming and giving instructions in case the cops came to scatter us with blows and shots in the air, as if we were little Martians from *Space Invaders*. We were kids. Not even fifteen. An army of kiddie aliens with painted-on charcoal mustaches, Lilliputians taking over the streets and the schools, shouting in shrill voices, clamoring, demanding the right to an independent student union, calling for school fees to be lowered, for our detained friends to be released, for the tyrant to be removed, for democracy to return, for the world to be more reasonable, for the future to arrive with no dark rooms, no screaming, no rats.

González didn't take part in our new guerrilla activities and intelligence work. I suppose she sat in the classroom writing those graph paper letters to Maldonado and telling her about things, like the trip she took with her father to Germany. González's father never quite recovered from the accident with the pin and the grenade, so the armed forces sent him to Germany for surgery on his left hand, which wasn't there anymore, to fix his stump. González went with him and saw the Berlin Wall, which divided the good guys from the bad guys and looked so much like the fence across our school yard behind the Virgen del Carmen. Of course, González stayed on the good guys' side, because the other side was dangerous and she wasn't allowed to go there. But after she got back from her trip, it was as if she'd crossed over to that other side, the bad guys' side, and she started to come to school in a red Chevy

Chevette, which was her father's, but was driven by Uncle Claudio, a kind of driver or bodyguard who looked out for her now. Uncle Claudio waited for her at the entrance to school, sitting in the red Chevy, smoking a cigarette, peering through his dark glasses, his mustache so much like the science teacher's, so much like the one the man who tortured people wore. When the bell rang at the end of the day, González appeared at the entrance, got in the car, and Uncle Claudio drove her home.

Some kids sat in the red Chevy and got to know Uncle Claudio. They said he was nice, he liked to kid around, and he'd even share his cigarettes with you. I once went for a drive around Parque O'Higgins with Uncle Claudio. González asked me to come, and Maldonado and I sat in the back seat with her. We got as far as El Pueblito and then we drove around the park for a long time. The Chevy was so nice and comfortable. Its blue leatherette seats were soft and shiny, and it smelled like mint from a little velvet sachet hanging on the turn signal. No one offered me cigarettes, but I have to say that it was a fun ride and Uncle Claudio, who watched us in the rearview mirror, was very polite and attentive, and he even opened the door for us when we got out of the car. González said that Uncle Claudio was a kind of assistant to her dad, they worked together, and since the country was such a mess right now, he kept an eye on her and drove her around, because her poor dad with his wooden left hand worked a lot and her mom had a little baby to nurse. So Uncle Claudio, with his tinted lenses and red Chevy, became part of the landscape of those years.

It was a time of Chevrolets and mustached men and men in dark glasses, too.

One March morning in 1985, we heard a disturbing report on the radio. The announcer described what he called a gruesome discovery. Three bodies had turned up with their throats slashed—*degollados*—on a bleak stretch of the road to Pudahuel Airport. Police and investigators were on their way to the scene, and so was the press. Reporters, photographers, TV cameras. The announcer spoke of surprise. Shock and surprise, as he put it. Everything was strange and puzzling, apparently, but what caught our attention was the word *degollados* because we didn't quite understand what it meant. I remember my mother explaining it to me in detail and the word turning up everywhere. We spotted it in newspaper headlines. We heard it on the radio, on TV, in conversations among parents, neighbors, teachers. The three bodies were identified at the Institute of Legal Medicine as José Manuel Parada, Manuel Guerrero, and Santiago Nattino. All three were Communist Party members, kidnapped a few days before. Parada and Guerrero were talking outside the entrance of a school like ours when they were seized. One was a dean and the other was a parent. Meters away were many students in their classrooms, Lilliputians like us, aliens with cork mustaches, all sitting at their desks, listening to the teacher of the moment, never imagining what was happening outside. A group of national police agents stopped traffic on the street, a helicopter hovered over the rooftops keeping watch, and a couple of cars, maybe Chevrolets with no license plates, parked at the entrance to the school. A group of men with mustaches and dark glasses got out and wrestled Parada and Guerrero into the car, just as they had taken José Weibel, Comrade Yuri, Contreras Maluje, the Flores brothers, and an endless list of other names. Some kids in gym class saw it all happening. That was the last anyone heard of Parada and Guerrero until they turned up with their throats slashed on the road to Pudahuel Airport.

It was a time of maimed, burnt, slashed, and bullet-ridden bodies, too.

The exact moment isn't clear to me, but I know that coffins and funerals and wreaths were suddenly everywhere, and there was no escaping them. Maybe it had always been that way and we were only just realizing it. Maybe we were distracted by all that history homework, all those assemblies, all those enactments of battles against the Peruvians. I remember attending the wake of one of the men whose throats were slashed. I remember a coffin, some place I'm not sure how I got to. There were several of us, all dressed in our uniforms. There were lots of flowers and candles and people standing in silence. At some point the son of one of the dead men appeared, a kid just like us, in his uniform, with his school crest, and he stood next to the coffin for a long time. Maybe he said something. I can't remember anymore, but what I know for sure is that he didn't cry. He didn't cry the whole time he was standing next to his father in that coffin. Then, another day, I remember a massive march toward the General Cemetery. Many voices shouting and chanting slogans, making demands, praying for the dead. The crowd tossing flower petals at the hearses, thousands of petals covering everything like a shower of flyers scattered in the street. The crowd advancing with flags and banners. We filled avenues, crossed bridges, walked on endlessly. But I don't know anymore whose funeral I'm remembering. It might be the Vergara brothers from Villa Francia, or the boy burned to death by a military patrol, or the priest shot in the settlement of La Victoria, or the boy riddled with bullets on Calle Bulnes, or the kidnapped reporter, or the group assassinated on the Feast of Corpus Christi, or one of the others, any of the others. Time isn't straightforward, it mixes everything up, shuffles the dead, merges them, separates them out again, advances backward, retreats in reverse, spins like a merry-go-round, like a tiny wheel in a laboratory cage, and traps us in funerals and marches and detentions, leaving us with no assurance of continuity or escape.

Days after we heard the word *degollados*, González stopped coming to class. We thought she was sick, but her absence stretched on for too long. Our teachers didn't tell us anything, and Maldonado had no idea what was happening either. González's phone didn't ring, her house was closed up, there was no way to get in touch with her. One day González was there, and the next she was gone, vanished from our lives. Without realizing it, we started getting used to the sight of her empty desk at the back of the classroom. When attendance was taken, we repeated her absence like a mantra. Elgueta, here. Fernández, here, González, absent. There were no more graph paper letters, no more Uncle Claudio, no more red Chevy, no more González. Eventually we were told that she had changed schools, she was at a German school, she had moved, her whole family was gone.

It was a time of disappearances and absences, too.

Long afterward, in 1994, when we were no longer at the school, when our uniforms no longer fit us and had been put away in some closet, the Chilean justice system delivered its first ruling on the kidnapping and murder of Communist Party members José Manuel Parada, Manuel Guerrero, and Santiago Nattino. The officers who committed the crime were sentenced to life in prison. On the same television screen where we used to play *Space Invaders*, we now saw the national police agents responsible for the murders. Six officers were involved. They appeared in plain sight. Their faces scrolled across the screen one after the other.

Though we had hardly known him, it wasn't hard to recognize him. His face, ten years older, told us nothing, but that poor little wooden hand in a black glove did. Next to him was Uncle Claudio of the red Chevy. El Pegaso, they called him. He said that he was following orders of his superior, Don Guillermo González Betancourt. He stated that he had stabbed one of the three men as his superior watched from the car, a red Chevette.

All of us saw him on the television screen. In some strange way we tuned in to the same image at the same time.

Sometimes I think about that drive I took with Maldonado and González to Parque O'Higgins. I think about the red Chevy. The blue leatherette seat, so soft and shiny. I imagine one of the three men sitting there, living the last minutes of his life on the road to Pudahuel Airport. I've tried to find information about which of the three rode in the Chevy, whether they were driven together or separately, whether they were in the back seat where I sat, or whether they were transported in the trunk, hidden and bound as I know they must have been, but as soon as I find it I forget again.

A while after that televised vision, one October morning in 1991, national police lieutenant Félix Sazo Sepúlveda enters the Crowne Plaza Hotel in the center of Santiago. The lieutenant rapidly approaches the Avis Rent-a-Car counter, behind which stands twenty-one-year-old Estrella González Jepsen, mother of his young son. Estrella is attending a customer when Lieutenant Sazo aims his service revolver at her. They've been separated for some time. The lieutenant has struggled to accept the fact of their separation. That's why he's been following her, harassing her over the phone, threatening her the way you'd threaten an enemy, an alien, a Communist Party member. Estrella, he shouts. Our classmate scarcely has time to look at him before she's struck by two bullets in the chest, one in the head, and a fourth in the back.

Like a little Martian from *Space Invaders* she flies apart into colored lights.

Estrella collapses in the fetal position, dying instantly. Police lieutenant Félix Sazo immediately shoots himself twice in the head with his smoking service revolver and falls to the ground.

On the same screen where we once watched *Lost in Space*, *Movie Nights*, *Sábado gigante*, and *The Twilight Zone*, our classmate turned up in the crime news.

And so this story comes to an end, with no mention of the man who tortured people, and with the image of Estrella González Jepsen dead at the hands of a national police officer. I imagine her in her school uniform, like the last time I saw her, in 1985. That's not how she looked when she died, of course, but it's how I want to imagine her. Beside her is the son of one of the *degollados*, just as I remember him at that wake, in his uniform, standing next to his father's coffin, not crying. The two of them in the same scene, where my mind wants to put them. Side by side, maybe looking at each other. Maybe not. They're the children. That's what they are.

We're all around them. Lying on the floor, in our uniforms too, but old now, gray-haired, balding, a few pounds heavier, careworn, fallen as in our enactments of the twenty-first of May on the deck of the enemy ship. Veterans of an old war. Little lead soldiers splashing in a fake sea of colored paper. The vast dark sea of the twilight zone.

I imagine him in a small apartment in a French town. Maybe not an apartment, a cabin. A simple place, in a village near the Swiss border. A sparsely populated area where the French police, who guard him, can monitor the comings and goings of any stranger. He's been here for just a few weeks. He's alone, he doesn't know a soul, and the neighbors speak an indecipherable language. He can't read the newspapers, can't understand what the news announcers or the bus driver or the grocer are saying. He has just started getting used to the coins, and though the village is small, he still loses his way on its streets. Like Colonel Cook from that old episode of *The Twilight Zone*, the man who tortured people has survived his voyage through space, but his odyssey through loneliness and fear is just beginning. He's an earthling lost on a strange planet. After taking the southern route out of Chile, he traveled on to Buenos Aires, and in Buenos Aires he got on a plane to Paris. He was there for a while, until Sécurité transferred him to this place that is now his. An unknown land, ruled by dead and untranslatable time.

It's hard for me to imagine him there.

Everything goes out of focus after he leaves Chile.

The words of the testimony he gave to the reporter and the lawyer are still here, doing their work, but the man who tortured people, as he once was, is beginning to fade. His mustache, the shape of his face, all of him, grows hazy, leached of color like those seventies snapshots from my childhood. I'm left with scraps, stray features from the photograph on the cover of *Cauce* magazine, which I pull up again now on my computer screen.

My face is reflected in the glass, my face merges with his.

I see myself behind him or maybe in front of him.

I look like a ghost in the picture.

A shadow lurking, a spy watching him though he doesn't know it.

That's what I am in part, I think: a spy watching him though he doesn't know it.

With some effort I imagine him eating breakfast one morning in his refuge. It's March 1985 and a few rays of winter sunshine come in through a small window. He butters a croissant at the café and goes through the motions of listening to the radio though he doesn't understand much, hardly anything at all. A news report is beginning. The man who tortured people knows this because he recognizes the theme music by now. The words are just sounds in the strange voice's unintelligible singsong. Suddenly he hears news from Chile being announced. He understands this perfectly well. *Rapport du Chili*. The man turns up the volume, as if by doing so he'll activate some instantaneous translation. He leans close to the speaker, and amid endless incomprehensible sentences he hears them foolishly repeating the word *égorgés*. *Égorgés*, says the announcer. *Égorgés*. And from listening to it over and over it stops being a sound and acquires character and weight.

Égorgés, he thinks to himself and he wonders what it means, just as we wondered when we heard the Spanish word for the first time, spoken in a Chilean announcer's voice, some hundreds of kilometers away. *Égorgés*, hears the man who tortured people, in that distant village where he's taken refuge, while in Chile, at the same time or moments before, the same word is being spoken on countless radios in Spanish: *degollados*.

The old raven shrieks in that window in France.

The man knows what it means.

It's March 29, 2016, and my friend Maldonado and I are walking down the street to a commemoration. It's the anniversary of the kidnapping of José Manuel Parada and Manuel Guerrero from the entrance of the Colegio Latinoamericano. In front of what used to be the school and is now the entrance to a modern apartment building, a memorial has been built in their name. The memorial also honors Santiago Nattino, who was kidnapped a day earlier from a different spot and was murdered along with his comrades.

As we walk, we think about González and the little letters she wrote to Maldonado when we were girls. We also think about the ride we took in González's red Chevy and about our random secret connection through her to the men we'll pay tribute to today. We walk on, remembering the intense times we were fated to grow up in, and as we do, a Billy Joel song gets stuck in my head. It's a song that M put on this afternoon when we were washing the dishes, something we kept singing and translating obsessively out of sheer joy. This happens to me sometimes. There are songs I can't shake, that stick around for days or even weeks in my unconscious. This is one of them. It's called "We Didn't Start the Fire," and it runs through a list of famous people in history, music, film, sports. Books are mentioned in it, too, and movies, TV series, events, anything that left its mark on the world from the day Joel was born to the moment he wrote the song in the late eighties. He rattles them all off in chronological order without explanation, but following along you get a picture of the world he grew up in.

> *Harry Truman, Doris Day, Red China, Johnnie Ray*
> *South Pacific, Walter Winchell, Joe DiMaggio*
> *Joe McCarthy, Richard Nixon, Studebaker, television*
> *North Korea, South Korea, Marilyn Monroe*
> *Rosenbergs, H-bomb, Sugar Ray, Panmunjom*
> *Brando, "The King and I" and "The Catcher in the Rye"*

So I go on talking to Maldonado and humming the chorus over and over without meaning to, as if I'm still in the kitchen washing dishes with M.

We didn't start the fire, no we didn't light it, but we tried to fight it.

On a different March 29, in a scene I've already imagined, the man who tortured people and his team kidnapped José Weibel from the bus he was riding with his family. The family was on its way to the very school that used to stand here, to drop off the children, like they did every morning. From the entrance to that school on another March 29, eleven years later, Guerrero and Parada would be taken to the same detention center where José was interrogated and tortured. Maybe by the very same agents. Maybe not. But they were part of the same group, the group of the man who tortured people.

Lots of people have arrived for the commemoration. The street has been closed off, a stage erected, and chairs set up, though too few for everyone who has come. Maldonado and I find a spot off to one side of the stage and try to catch up with the ceremony, which has already begun. A presenter explains how the memorial was planned, speaks about how some in the neighborhood were opposed to it, and addresses the objections of municipal officials. As we listen, I see one of José Weibel's children in the distance. I recognize him because he's a well-known reporter, an investigative journalist. Around this time, he's just published a book exposing the misappropriation of public funds by the Chilean army under democracy. Scandalous sums disappearing as if by magic. Weibel Junior is sitting up front, with his wife and children. He must be about my age, or a little older. He's speaking animatedly with Manuel Guerrero's son. They're laughing in the way that good friends do. A strange thread of coincidences link their lives to this day and this corner.

Guerrero Senior must have recognized the place he was brought to on March 29, 1985. From the school, he and Parada were transported to a facility called La Firma, where Weibel Senior also ended up on a different March 29, in 1976. Guerrero Senior had been there around the same time, and survived. The man who tortured people says that he took part in that earlier detention as well. The man who tortured people says that Manuel Guerrero was picked up in Departamental and then taken to La Firma. With a feeling of déjà vu, Guerrero must have remembered that previous detention and his stay at La Firma in 1976. Having been there before in the hands of the same people, he may have thought he'd be better at surviving it this time. Having gotten out once, maybe he thought he could get out again. But the twilight zone stop-watch is remorseless. No matter the year or the day, its tiny hands keep time locked up inside it, revolving around itself, advancing backward, retreating forward, inevitably ending up in the same spot, that place beyond rescue distance where José Weibel landed, and then Guerrero, Parada, and Nattino, eleven years later. The strange thread of coincidences running through these two stories of kidnappings, children, parents, and death runs through everything from that time, I believe, and it stitches us here, on this street corner where we're taking part in a commemoration.

A group of children is singing on stage. They're out of tune, and they start over. In the crowd across the street, I see my friend X and her little girl L. I also spot F and his mother, who got chairs and are now listening in comfort, while at the back I think I see little S on the shoulders of her father, N. Circling the stage with their cameras, my documentarian friends are filming, working on a movie about Guerrero Junior. There are many familiar faces on this corner. I could name H, R, C, E, a whole alphabet, the full roster of a class, meeting here tonight. Several I don't even known by name, but I recognize them from other ceremonies like this, other vigils, old marches, their faces stuck in my faulty memory just like this dumb song I can't get out of my head.

We didn't start the fire, no we didn't light it, but we tried to fight it.

The man who tortured people says he doesn't regret having talked. The man who tortured people says he doesn't regret turning up at the reporter's office that August morning so long ago. Since then, his life hasn't been easy. Hidden away in his French refuge, he's been besieged by rats and ravens. I know that in France he's met with many people. I know Sécurité has transported him to Paris each time anyone requested his testimony. He has arranged meeting times, trips, secret appointments. I know that he has spotted enemies, I know that more than once he's had to flee, victim of paranoia or real persecution. I know that he has continued to identify photographs. I know he's met with lawyers, judges, victims' family members. He even returned to Chile to testify in court not long ago. Which means that for thirty years, his dedication to bearing witness has been unwavering. Despite the fear, the paranoia, and the distance, he'd do the same thing all over again, he says. If time went mad the way it did back then and stopped and turned backward, putting him in the same situation, he'd do it again.

But there is one thing that troubles his conscience about the testimony he gave, he says. Something he'd try to change or handle more carefully to prevent collateral damage. He'd try to keep the thread on which he strung his words from getting tangled up in the names of Parada, Guerrero, and Nattino.

Parada's daughter and Guerrero's son take the stage. She looks a lot like her father; he looks like his. Both of them thank the memorial project on behalf of their families. The organizers are a collective of young people who probably weren't even born when it all happened. Guerrero Junior reads a letter that his own daughter sent from Europe, where she's in school. It's a message for everyone, because she doesn't want to be absent despite the distance. She talks about the legacy that ties her to this corner and about the challenge of keeping memory alive. As Guerrero Junior reads the letter, I think that this memorial and this whole ceremony are for her. Not for her grandfather and his friends, not for her parents, not for us, but for her and for the children in the choir. For Weibel Junior's children. For L, X's little girl. For S who is watching it all from N's shoulders. For my own son, who isn't with me today, tired of tagging along to memorials like this one.

While the man who tortured people was speaking with the reporter, the reporter knew the information was extremely delicate. Which is why she decided to confirm every tiny detail of his testimony before it was published. So she contacted her friend José Manuel Parada, fellow Communist Party member and manager of the Vicariate of Solidarity's Department of Documentation and Archives. He was the best person to help her analyze the interview material because he knew more than almost anybody about the apparatus of repression. Every day, José Manuel Parada received accounts of kidnapping, torture, disappearance, and other abuses. He suggested bringing in Manuel Guerrero, whom he trusted implicitly and who could triangulate the interview information with his own experience of being detained by the team of the man who tortured people. Who better to help than someone who had been there and survived?

Sunk in that dark zone, the three analyzed the long hours of recorded testimony. They spent months navigating the weighty, burdened words of the man who tortured people. Each document was strung on a sticky thread that clung to their bodies, entangling them. Everything that this messenger from the far side of the mirror had brought over from the troubling place he inhabited seemed to be entirely true. The reporter, Parada, and Guerrero went about connecting the dots, recognizing beloved names on the list of the dead, linking the crimes described to other crimes, using the material to reconstruct scenes of detention, torture, execution, guessing at the identity of the agents behind each nickname, making the pieces fit, untangling a skein that even now is hard to follow.

Once the information had been checked, the reporter, along with Guerrero and Parada, decided that the interview would be offered to the *Washington Post*, in the United States, and later delivered in full to the Chilean courts. This had to wait until the man who tortured people had left the country and was safe, that was the agreement. Until then, his words transcribed from the dark zone would keep all of them—their team, the lawyer, the man who tortured people—dangling from a single thread.

We've been here for almost an hour and the presenter is beginning to draw things to a close. Family members, officials, and a few singers have all had their turn on stage. The inauguration ceremony is coming to an end, but an invitation is extended after the speeches and words of affection, the same invitation that is extended every March 29: the moment has come to light the candles. Now it's clearer where to do it; instead of a long line of untidy little flames speckling the street with their melted wax, there will be an organized blaze around the memorial. Whether authorized or unauthorized, outside an apartment building or at the entrance to a small school, a small gathering or a huge group like this one: every March 29, this corner is the same again.

One day a priest turned up at the reporter's office. I imagine him in a long cassock, sitting across the desk, speaking slowly, with the kind of fixed smile on his face often seen on men of the cloth. The priest said that he had come on behalf of the family of the man who tortured people. The priest said that the man's family members knew he had talked to her, and that he hadn't been home since. Given the circumstances, he was asking for a little compassion for the wife and children of the man who tortured people. Given the circumstances, our priest was requesting a clue to his whereabouts.

The reporter—I know this, I'm not imagining it—had no idea where the man who tortured people was. For her own safety, she knew nothing about anything that happened to him before he left the country. The meeting in the Plaza Santa Ana, the drive in the Renault van past the detention centers, his hiding place on church property, his attempts to acquire a passport, his southern route out of the country to Argentina, all of the scenes I've been trying to imagine: none of it was information to which the reporter had access.

She apologized to the priest and said she had no idea what he was asking about. She didn't know any Andrés Antonio Valenzuela Morales, she said. So there was no way she could give any information about his whereabouts. The fake priest's response was to pull a gun out from under his cassock: Listen, cunt. Tell us where he is or you'll be sorry.

Everyone has gathered around the memorial. Stage, chairs, and microphones are left behind. We've fallen out of line as everyone tries to find a space to light a candle for each of the three honorees. A little flicker for Guerrero, another for Parada, and a final one for Nattino. Maldonado and I haven't brought candles or lighters, but we watch it all and we're part of the ritual, camouflaged among those who've come prepared. Across from us, a little girl asks her mother if this is a birthday party, if that's why people are lighting candles. Her mother laughs and doesn't answer, while Maldonado and I watch as more and more candles are added to the big cake.

It's December 1984 and the reporter is meeting a trusted friend. He is traveling to the United States and she has asked him to carry a complicated document for her. For his own protection, she can't tell him what it is, but someone will contact him to receive it once he reaches the United States. He has accepted the mission. Back then, this is what true friends did, so I imagine the reporter sewing up the lining of her friend's coat, because that's where she's hidden the interview with the man who tortured people. The interview is to be delivered to the *Washington Post*, to be published at some future date.

Days or maybe hours later, I don't know, the reporter's friend gets on a plane. He settles into his seat, and after he fastens his seat belt he begins to feel a strange sensation against his back, around his kidneys. It's a mild but rather irksome warmth, accompanied by his friend's voice. Don't take the papers out of your coat, he hears her saying in his head. Don't read them, the less you know the better, for your sake and everyone else's. And the plane takes off, leaving Chilean soil, and he again feels a pressing against his back. Now it's an unsettling twitching inside his coat, which he hasn't taken off and doesn't plan to take off. It's as if he's transporting an animal, a living creature pacing back and forth inside its cage. After a while, the stewardess brings him something to eat. He uncovers the meal on the tray, helping himself with his metal utensils to rice, salad, noodles, meat, or whatever he's been served, feeling the disturbing presence and thinking again that he mustn't take the document out of the lining of his coat, mustn't read it. And he eats. And he drinks wine from his glass. And then it's time for coffee and the stewardess takes the tray, but he decides to keep the little metal knife. Before anyone notices, he tucks it into the same coat that he knows he shouldn't unstitch. Don't remove the papers from the lining, that's what he was told. Don't read them. And feeling that stifling warmth against his back, he drinks his coffee and thinks about the creature he's harboring. It's a dangerous beast, no doubt, something like a rat or a raven, he feels it there against his kidneys, and now it's between his shoulder blades. And then he orders a whiskey. And another and another. Or maybe he doesn't order anything. Maybe alcohol is no distraction and all at once he rebels. He simply can't stand the presence of whatever it is against his back anymore and he stops listening to the annoying little voice telling him what he can and can't do. Like in a children's story, the protagonist is tempted to disobey his mother's orders, or his father's, or his older brother's, whoever has forbidden him to do something, and with the little metal knife from his meal he unstitches the coat's lining and removes the document, just as he's been told not to do, and rats and ravens are coming out of the papers, and he's horrified and afraid and he doesn't want the ink of this cursed text to taint him, but it's too late now, now he's stained, now he can't help it and he reads, just as he was told not to do, and as he does, the words of the man who tortured people come sticky and dense out of Pandora's box, all the threads tangled up with Parada, Guerrero, and Nattino's names.

The reporter's friend can't believe what he's reading.

The reporter's friend weeps silently, steadily, there in the airplane seat.

So many familiar names, so many deaths, such horror.

The reporter's friend clings to the seat belt, because he knows that once he's done reading he'll tumble into space and never be the same again.

I remember another episode of *The Twilight Zone*. In it, a lonely man of few means finds a book with an inscription forbidding anyone to read it on fear of death. Of course the man is tempted to open it and read what's inside, but first he wants to test whether the warning is true. The man wordlessly passes the book to an old acquaintance, and right away the man starts to read it. What he finds there is riveting, and he reads and reads for hours until at last he falls down dead with a big smile on his face.

The man who found the book is shaken. Not satisfied by what he's seen, he tempts fate again and gives the book to another acquaintance. The very same thing happens again. The second acquaintance can't stop reading and he reads and reads in delight until he falls dead with the same smile on his face as the first reader.

The man who found the cursed book begins to use it as a weapon against his enemies. If anyone tries to collect money from him, if anyone opposes his ideas, the book comes to the rescue. Everyone reads and falls down dead, and his life is gradually transformed and ruled by this seductive, deadly book.

The man who found the cursed book becomes a millionaire, owner of a chain of stores and a palatial house where he lives with his four children and his platinum blond wife. One day, always careful and paranoid about where the book is hidden, he decides to take it out of its safe and bury it in a secret spot in his big yard. What the man fails to predict is that one of his four children is watching from the bedroom window.

One day the man comes home and no one is there to greet him. The children don't come running with hugs and kisses, and his platinum blond wife is nowhere to be seen. The servants take his coat and hat. When he goes up to his room he finds his whole family lying on the big bed. His wife has the book open in her hands and the children, gathered around her, seem to be listening intently to a long story. But no one is listening anymore. No one is reading. The man's family are resting in peace, with smiles on their faces. Whatever they've read has transported them once and for all to the dark realms of the twilight zone.

The reporter's friend disembarks for a layover in Caracas, Venezuela, with the document hidden in the lining of his coat. He walks out of the airport and there he is welcomed by a group of friends who realize at once that something is wrong. The reporter's friend can't keep the document secret, and he talks. And out of his mouth come the heavy words of the man who tortured people. And out of his mouth come rats and ravens. And the tale captivates and consumes all who hear it. A Chilean reporter who is part of the group decides to publish the interview in Caracas. No permission is requested, no notice given; the testimony is simply published immediately in a Venezuelan newspaper.

What comes next is like that episode from *The Twilight Zone*.

Words written in dangerous ink turn against their owner.

Words written in poisonous ink turn against whoever reads them.

When word of its publication gets out, the group of the man who tortured people tires of searching for him and decides to destroy everything. They wipe out the publishing arm of AGECH, the Chilean Teachers' Union, because they're sure that the originals of the published testimony must be there. The press is registered in the name of a graphic designer named Santiago Nattino. That same day he is kidnapped and taken to La Firma. They handcuff him to a metal bed frame, where the interrogations and torture begin. The next day, March 29, 1985, a day like today, they follow another strand of the investigation. Another detainee, in the middle of another torture session, in another clandestine headquarters, has declared he knew that his party comrades José Manuel Parada and Manuel Guerrero were working to analyze the testimony of a security agent. Following that thread, the group of the man who tortured people makes its way to this corner, this very spot, and early in the morning, with all the children in their classrooms, with Guerrero and Parada's own children beginning the school day, the two men are abducted from an entrance that no longer exists, and they're taken to La Firma to be tortured day and night.

They must have been asked about the man who tortured people.
They must have been ordered to reveal his whereabouts.

On March 30, 1985, as everyone is looking for them, as the press is talking about the kidnapping, in a caravan headed by the old red Chevy that I once rode in with Maldonado, a commando unit takes the three detainees down the airport road. The comrades of the man who tortured people are there. González, the officer with the wooden hand who was my classmate's father, is there. The cars stop and the comrades of the man who tortured people make the three detainees get out. With a knife they cut their throats and leave them to bleed to death. The country wakes up to this "gruesome discovery," that's how I heard the news on my mother's car radio on the way to school. That's what I remember the voice of the announcer saying, the same person who is the presenter at today's ceremony, which will never end.

There was a video of the Billy Joel song. In it, Joel is drumming on the kitchen table when suddenly a couple comes in. It's a bride and groom straight out of the 1950s, who are about to begin their life together. They don't see Joel. He's like a ghost from the future watching them unseen, witness to everything that happens in the kitchen. Soon a child appears, the couple's son. And then the boy grows up, becomes an adolescent and then a young man as styles change, the kitchen appliances grow more modern, and the parents' clothing evolves. A whole life unfolds in that kitchen. Birthdays, graduations, parties, lunches, Christmases, funerals. Sometimes we see newspaper headlines. Sometimes *Life* magazine is read. Elvis appears in a photograph. Calendar pages fly off, one month after another, and clocks spin madly. And sometimes the family is a different family. Because families are all alike and each era leaves its mark on families and kitchens, whether they know it or not. And sometimes, in the chorus, Joel keeps drumming on the table, but behind him the kitchen is gone, and instead there's a kind of window though which we see images from his times, from the world in which he was fated to grow up. A man hanging from chains in a tree, which makes me think of Korea. An Asian man shooting another man, which makes me think of Vietnam. Arrests, policemen, soldiers, bodies from some war. And then flames start to come in through the window to the place where Joel is. Flames that burn everything up, because there has never been a kitchen anywhere in the world that is safe from the blaze of history.

Coup in Chile.
President Allende dies at La Moneda.
Mass arrests,
secret executions,
war tribunals.
The Caravan of Death travels south and north.
Víctor Jara is tortured

and killed at the National Stadium.
The man who tortured people starts at AGA.
Our neighbors, the Quevedos,
hide flyers at our house.
My grandmother, alarmed, makes a fuss.

Creation of DINA, the National Intelligence Directorate.
Creation of SIFA, the Air Force Intelligence Service.
Selective detentions, abductions,
people disappeared.
The man who tortured people
joins an antisubversive group.
I start school, wearing a uniform for the first time
and carrying a metal lunch box.

Assassination of General Carlos Prats,
ex–minister of the interior under Salvador Allende.
His car explodes in Buenos Aires.
On Calle Santa Fe, MIR leader Miguel Enríquez is killed.
Pinochet flies to Franco's funeral.
The Vicariate of Solidarity is created.
Bodies in the Cajón del Maipo, fingers missing the first
joints,
no fingerprints.

Assassination of Orlando Letelier in Washington.
Ceremony on Cerro Chacarillas,
seventy-six young men climbing the hill with torches,
receiving medals from Pinochet.
The man who tortured people

becomes a guard at clandestine detention centers.
El Chapulín Colorado
makes an appearance at the National Stadium,
I go to see him, bringing my plastic squeaky hammer, the
chipote chillón.

Contreras Maluje is kidnapped blocks from my house,
My mother watches it happen and then
tells us the story at lunchtime.
El Quila Leo is assassinated.
The man who tortured people
cries secretly in his barracks.

DINA is dissolved and CNI, the National Information
Center, is created.
The first bodies of the disappeared
are discovered in the Lonquén mines.
Don Francisco hosts the first Telethon,
I have a sleepover with a group of friends
and we stay up all night to watch it.

Family members of the disappeared chain themselves
to the gates of the National Congress.
Six-year-old Rodrigo Anfruns is kidnapped,
and we're all afraid of being kidnapped
whether we're blond like Rodrigo or not.

A national plebiscite is held.
The new constitution is approved,
the one that governs us to this day.

Pinochet moves to La Moneda.
Fire at the Torre Santa María.
The Apumanque mall opens.
Ex-president Eduardo Frei is assassinated
at the Clínica Santa María.
Union leader Tucapel Jiménez is assassinated.
Opposition magazines begin to circulate
among my classmates.
I read the special issue on torture and dream about rats.

Economic crisis in Chile.
My Uncle R and Aunt M leave for Miami, fleeing their
debts.
The Parque Arauco mall opens.
Family members of the disappeared
Light candles in front of the cathedral,
I see the little flames go out
in jets from the water cannons.

First national protest.
Santiago governor Carol Urzúa dies
in an ambush.
Five MIR members gunned down in retaliation
on Calle Janequeo and Calle Fuenteovejuna.
My mother-in-law locks the door
when she hears the shots.
M hears it all from the thirteenth floor.
The man who tortured people
comes home with bloodstained pants.
His wife notices.

The Manuel Rodríguez Patriotic Front
commences its activities
with a first general blackout,
my grandmother buys candles by the dozen.

New national protest.
Stones thrown at Pinochet in Punta Arenas.
Family members of the disappeared
light candles in front of the cathedral,
I see the little flames go out
in another jet from the water cannons.
The man who tortured people
arrives at the *Cauce* magazine offices.
I want to talk, he says.

Priest André Jarlan is killed
in the settlement of La Victoria.
The man who tortured people
takes refuge on Catholic Church property.
His superiors search for him.
State of siege declared,
opposition press banned.
The man who tortured people leaves Chile.
The man who tortured people seeks asylum in France.
Los Prisioneros launch *La voz de los ochenta*.
New earthquake in the Zona Central.

Brothers Rafael and Eduardo Vergara Toledo
are killed by a national police patrol.
On the road to Pudahuel Airport,

Santiago Nattino, Manuel Guerrero, and José Manuel Parada
are found with their throats slit.
We go to their wake, we go to their burial.
New national protest.
We scatter flyers in the center of Santiago.
We see a headline on the cover of *Cauce* magazine
that reads I TORTURED PEOPLE,
we decide that the torturer
looks like our science teacher.

Back to the Future is released.
Marty McFly breaks the barriers of time
and space and travels to the past.
Halley's Comet passes.
A psychic claims to speak
to the Virgin in Peñablanca.
In France, the man who tortured people keeps speaking out
from his hiding place.
New national protest,
we scatter more leaflets in the center of Santiago.

The young photographer Rodrigo Rojas de Negri
is burned to death by an army patrol.
Vigils, days of reflection, marches.

Sábado gigante debuts in the U.S.
Attempted assassination of Pinochet
by the Manuel Rodríguez Patriotic Front,
Pinochet escapes and claims to have seen the Virgin.

The reporter Pepe Carrasco is assassinated.
In France, the man who tortured people keeps speaking out
from his hiding place.

The pope visits Chile.
We go to the National Stadium to see him,
we go to Parque O'Higgins to see him.
Stones are thrown at us and we're drenched in water and
tear gas.
Cecilia Bolocco is crowned Miss Universe.
Twelve members of the Manuel Rodríguez Patriotic Front
die in Operation Albania.
Vigils, protests, marches.
Meetings of the student movement Pro Feses
in a warehouse on Calle Serrano.

Seventy-seven actors receive death threats.
Superman visits Chile in support of his fellow thespians.
We go to see him at the Matucana Warehouse.
The mother of a classmate is kidnapped.
Days later she turns up with her nipples sliced
by a razor blade.
In France, the man who tortured people keeps speaking out
from his hiding place.

Family members of the disappeared
light more and more candles in front of the cathedral.

The Coalition of Parties for NO is created.
The poet Enrique Lihn dies.

Pinochet is declared candidate for president.
The NO campaign begins.
The YES campaign begins.
Marches, rallies, water cannons, detentions.
Plebiscite in Chile.
Vote YES for the regime to stand.
Vote NO for the regime to end.
NO wins.

Family members of the disappeared
light candles in front of the cathedral.

I enroll
at the Universidad Católica's Theater School.
Rod Stewart sings at the National Stadium.
Cóndor Rojas cuts his own forehead
at the Maracanã Stadium.
MIR leader Jécar Neghme
is shot and killed on Calle Bulnes.
The Berlin Wall falls.
Back to the Future II is released.
Marty McFly breaks the barriers of time
and space and travels to the year 2015 to save his
children.
Family members of the disappeared
light candles in front of the cathedral.

Presidential elections.
Patricio Aylwin Azócar, candidate of the Coalition of
Parties for Democracy, wins.

Celebration of democracy at the National Stadium.
A group of us get tickets and go together.

Family members of the disappeared
light candles in front of the cathedral.
They're sure that now they'll learn
the whereabouts of their family members.

Congress is back in session.
David Bowie concert at the National Stadium.
I meet the Thin White Duke and want to be like him.
Amnesty International organizes two concerts.
I see Sinéad O'Connor live
and want to be like her too.
Months later I decide to shave my head.

The remains of Salvador Allende
are moved to the General Cemetery
with state honors.
Spectacular rescue
of Marco Ariel Antonioletti of the Lautarista Youth
Movement
from Sótero del Río Hospital.
Hours later he is shot in the forehead and killed
by PDI assault troops
at the house of Coalitionist Juan Carvajal.
Army placed on alert in response to investigation
of the *pinocheques*, illegal checks paid out to Pinochet's son.
Three thousand five hundred and fifty counts

of human rights violations
are documented in the Rettig Report.
President Patricio Aylwin
asks the forgiveness of victims' families
for the abuses.
He announces that justice will be done
to the extent possible.

Family members of the disappeared
light candles in front of the cathedral.
They're still waiting for word
about the whereabouts of their family members.

Back to the Future III is released.
Marty McFly breaks the barriers of time and space
and travels to the past to try to correct the future.

The Patriotic Front assassinates Jaime Guzmán
at the Eastern Campus gate
of the Universidad Católica.
We see it all from the bus stop.

Fiestas Spandex at the Esmeralda Theater.
The Patriotic Front kidnaps Cristián Edwards,
son of the owner of *El Mercurio*.
Two Patriotic Front members are gunned down
when they leave the house where they're holding a family
hostage.
It all happens on the corner by my school.

Erich Honecker and his wife Margot
arrive requesting asylum.
Sor Teresa de Los Andes is canonized.
Boinazo near La Moneda:
army troops muster in combat uniform
protesting the opening of the *pinocheques* case again.
Family members of the disappeared
light candles in front of the cathedral.
There are no more water cannons, but still no answers.

Three Lautaristas are killed
on the bus on which they escaped after an attack.
The police kill three passengers and wound twelve.
Eduardo Frei Jr. wins the presidential elections.
Kurt Cobain commits suicide in Seattle.
The Memorial of Disappeared and Executed Persons is
inaugurated.

Family members of the disappeared
light candles in front of the cathedral.

Rolling Stones in concert at the National Stadium.
M and I take our backpacks
and set off around the world.
Writer José Donoso dies at seventy-one.
Spectacular escape of four members
of the Patriotic Front
from the high-security prison.
A helicopter carries them away through the skies
dangling in a basket.

Asian financial crisis. Chile survives because we are
the jaguars of South America.
More malls, more billboards,
more credit cards.
More options to buy everything on the installment plan.

Family members of the disappeared
light candles in front of the cathedral.

Pinochet cedes command of the army
and becomes a senator for life in the National Congress.
The world laughs at Chilean democracy.
The Communist Party
files the first lawsuit against Pinochet.
El Chino Ríos becomes the top-ranked tennis player in
the world.

Pinochet is arrested in London.
The Chilean government intervenes on his behalf,
asking for his release.
The world laughs at Chilean democracy.

Family members of the disappeared
light candles in front of the cathedral.

Pinochet appears before a British court.
We follow it all via artists' sketches
because no media are allowed in the English courts.
My grandmother dies just before her ninetieth
birthday.

Cardinal Silva Henríquez, creator of the Vicariate of
Solidarity, dies.
Jack Straw decides to release Pinochet
on grounds of ill health.
Pinochet returns to Chile in a Chilean air force plane.
He rises from his wheelchair,
bursting with health,
to salute the head of the army, who is there to greet him.
The world laughs at Chilean democracy.

Family members of the disappeared
light candles in front of the cathedral.

Ricardo Lagos takes office as president of the republic.
A military-civilian forum, Mesa de Diálogo, is
established.
The fate of two hundred of the disappeared is reported on
national television.

Family members of the disappeared
light candles in front of the cathedral.
Names are missing, they say.
Whereabouts are missing.
They keep asking: Where are they?

Judge Juan Guzmán Tapia
requests the impeachment of Pinochet
in order to strip him of his immunity as senator for life
and make him face some of the eighty-odd lawsuits filed
against him.

M and I become the parents of a boy called D.
Attack on the Twin Towers.
D eats his first baby cereal
as we watch the towers fall on TV.

The National Commission on Political Prisoners
 and Torture delivers the Valech Report
with the testimony of more than thirty-five thousand
Chileans who were detained and subjected to torture.

Family members of the disappeared
light candles in front of the cathedral.
Still asking.
Still waiting.

D takes his first steps and starts nursery school.
Roberto Bolaño dies in Vall d'Hebrón Hospital in
Barcelona.
The Supreme Court upholds Pinochet's impeachment.
Former DINA director Manuel Contreras is arrested.
His daughter cries and writhes on the ground.
Contreras resists arrest.

Family members
of the disappeared
light candles
in front of the cathedral.

Beginning of the Revolución Pingüina,
a student movement across Chile.

Sit-ins, marches, hunger strikes
demanding improvements
in public education.

Hunger strike by Mapuche activists held at Angol Prison
demanding communal property rights.
Militarization of Mapuche communities.
Application of antiterrorism laws
created by the Pinochet government.

Family
members
of
the
disappeared
light
candles
at
the
cathedral.

Surrounded by family and loved ones,
Augusto Pinochet dies at the army hospital
aged ninety-one.
He never served a sentence in Chile.
I hear the news and get into an accident on the highway.
The next day I visit my insurance company.
It's next door to the Military School
where Pinochet is lying pompously in state.
Thousands of fanatics weep

and stand in line to bid the tyrant farewell.
The grandson of General Prats
patiently stands in line.
Hours later, he reaches the coffin and spits on it.

We didn't start the fire, no we didn't light it, but we tried to fight it.

I smell the candles burning on the corner. I recognize the smoke clinging to my skin, my hair, my faulty memory. Unsettling stink of burned tires, paraffin, barricades, hundreds of lit candles. All these years and it's still impossible to shake it. Time stands still. Present, future, and past blur together in this ceremony, a parenthesis of smoke governed by the stopwatch from *The Twilight Zone*. I imagine there must be other children, like the children of José Weibel, Manuel Guerrero, José Manuel Parada, and Santiago Nattino, hidden among the candle flames. Maybe Yuri Gahona is here with his sister, Evelyn. Maybe they're still playing with their father's white bishop. Maybe Alexandra is here too: little Smurfette, Lucía Vergara's daughter. Maybe she's come with her own daughter and her daughter's partner, because I know they're the mothers of a little girl. Maybe Quila Leo's children are here. Maybe Carol Flores's children are here. Maybe Arturo Villavela's children are here. Hugo Ratier's children. Maybe Mario is here, the boy who lost the house in Janequeo that wasn't his house and the family that wasn't his family. The boy who was given asylum in Sweden and started a real family there. Maybe he's back again with his real wife and children and they're all here somewhere, joining in the festivities, breathing the sticky smoke from all these candles.

I look around for the little girl whose mother never answered her question. I try to find her, because I want to tell her yes, this is a birthday party, the way she imagined. We've been celebrating this strange day and lighting and lighting these damn candles for too long. For an endless, tedious moment of déjà vu, we play the parenthesis game and we're always here in the fragile light of the little flames, our eyes red from the smoke. I search for the girl amid all these people I know because I want to tell her she's right, this is a party, but a shitty party. We don't deserve birthdays like this. We never deserved them. Not her, not me. Not Maldonado, not X and his little girl L, or F and his mother, or N and little S, or M, or D, or Alexandra, or Mario, or Yuri, or Evelyn, or anybody's children, anybody's grandchildren.

I want to tell her this, but I can't find her.

She isn't here anymore.

Maldonado takes my arm the way she used to when we were kids and we pretended to be old ladies. I lean on her and she leans on me and we inhale deeply, sucking in all the air and smoke that our worn-out lungs can hold, and when we're about to burst, we whisper our wishes and blow as hard as we can. We blow with the force of someone spitting on a coffin, trying once and for all to extinguish the fire of all the candles on this shitty cake.

There's one last scene that I want to write. It isn't part of any imaginative exercise, but pure domestic reality. In this scene, water sloshes in the dishwasher as M and I scrub the day's grime from the tile floor. M is talking about *Frankenstein*. He's been rereading the book and now he remembers that at the end Mary Shelley's monster goes to hide in the Arctic, far from the world, fleeing himself and the crimes he's committed. He's a monster, M says. He alone knows the horror of what he's done, so he decides to disappear.

As I rinse the forks and spoons, I think it's true, the monster is a monster. But there is a qualification: He didn't choose to be what he is. He was part of a gruesome experiment. Doctor Frankenstein stitched a body out of corpses and brought to life a being haunted by its own smell of death.

M, scrubbing the dirty frying pan with steel wool, replies that this explains his actions, but it doesn't absolve him of having been a monster. According to that logic, all monsters would be exonerated by their pasts.

I imagine the white landscape of the Arctic and a half-beast, half-human creature wandering the emptiness, condemned to loneliness and a smell he'll never shed because it's a part of him. The monster repented, I insist. That's why he hides away in the Arctic. Doesn't that mean something?

It might, says M. But that only makes him a repentant monster.

Dear Andrés,
in this new life of yours
that I find so hard to imagine,
maybe you don't hide the way you used to.

Thirty years are enough
to learn how to blend in.
Probably by now you're part of the landscape.
Probably your Chilean-accented French
doesn't attract much attention anymore.
Probably this letter from me
written in your native language,
in short, curt sentences like yours,
will strike you as a message
in some indecipherable tongue.

I know your mustache is gray now.
I know you wear glasses.
I know your wife from back then is no longer your wife.
I know you're in touch with your children and grandchildren.
I know you've had different jobs.
I know you drive a truck.
I know you're sick, or you were.
I know that in the evenings you read and forage for
mushrooms.
I know that Chile has faded somewhat in your mind,
but not your beach: Papudo.

Dear Andrés, Papudo is still a pretty beach.
Especially now in winter

when only a few of us are strolling
its black sands.
In this life, which is the only one I have,
I've chosen this place to say goodbye.
Ahead of me a dog runs alone,
fleeing the waves.
It barks and startles a flock of gulls.
The sea is tossed by the wind.
It comes and goes, like the scenes I've tried to imagine.

I hear voices each time a wave breaks.
Cries for help trapped in glass bottles.
Hundreds of bottles.
Maybe more.

In the distance I think I see you smoking a cigarette.
You're young, no mustache,
probably not in military service yet.
You must be a few years older than my son.
You've stopped for a moment and you're staring at the
horizon
as if you know that over there, across the sea,
a hiding place awaits you and becomes your home.

As you smoke you're interrupted by someone's intrusive
stare.
It's me, spying on you from the future.
You wave politely.
You smile, I think, and walk on along the shore.
You don't know who I am.

You can't imagine the message I bring
from Christmases future.

The air is cool here in Papudo.
I'll eat clams and dip my feet in the icy sea.
But that will be tomorrow, it's getting dark already
and the stars are beginning to come out.

Dear Andrés,
in your new life of foraging for mushrooms
and reading in the evenings,
you're probably in bed,
awake or asleep, dreaming of rats.
Of dark rooms and rats.
Of women and men screaming,
of letters from the future inquiring about those
screams.

When I was a girl I was told that stars
were the bonfires of the dead.
I didn't understand why the dead
lit bonfires.
I assumed it was to send smoke signals.
How else could they communicate
with no phone, no mail?

My fire has gone out here on the beach.
I'm a hazy shadow in the glow of the embers.
I pick up a piece of charcoal
and draw on a dark mustache.

It's something I learned as a girl.
I was trained for this, I think.

Born to be a detective and a seer.

The smoke reddens my eyes.
I move in an army crawl, eyes watering,
across Papudo's black sands.
On hands and knees I reach your pillow.
I creep into your slumbers and with a curved knife
I write the words you've dictated to me
so that they echo
like smoke signals sent into infinity.

This is an information post, a smoke station.

Of shared nightmares.
Of dark rooms.
Of stopped clocks.
Of twilight zones.
Of rats and ravens still shrieking.
Of mustaches painted on with soot.

And the future will come
and it will have the red eyes of a devil dreaming.

You're right.
Nothing is real enough for a ghost.

Papudo, V Region, June 2016

Nona Fernández was born in Santiago, Chile, in 1971. She is an actress and writer, and has published two plays, a collection of short stories, a work of nonfiction, and six novels, including *Space Invaders*. In 2016 she was awarded the Premio Sor Juana Inés de la Cruz. Her books have been translated into French, Italian, German, Greek, Portuguese, Turkish, and English.

Natasha Wimmer is the translator of nine books by Roberto Bolaño, including *The Savage Detectives* and *2666*. Her most recent translations are Nona Fernández's *Space Invaders* and *Sudden Death* by Álvaro Enrigue. She lives in Brooklyn with her husband and two children.

The text of *The Twilight Zone* is set in Arno Pro.
Book design by Rachel Holscher.
Composition by Bookmobile Design and Digital Publisher
Services, Minneapolis, Minnesota.
Manufactured by Versa Press on acid-free,
30 percent postconsumer wastepaper.